Alice Gardner

Rome

the middle of the world

Alice Gardner

Rome
the middle of the world

ISBN/EAN: 9783337382605

Printed in Europe, USA, Canada, Australia, Japan

Cover: Foto ©Andreas Hilbeck / pixelio.de

More available books at **www.hansebooks.com**

ROME
THE MIDDLE OF THE WORLD

BY

ALICE GARDNER

Historical Lecturer of Newnham College, Cambridge

AUTHOR OF "JULIAN THE PHILOSOPHER," "FRIENDS OF THE OLDEN TIME," ETC.

EDWARD ARNOLD

London
37, BEDFORD STREET

New York
70, FIFTH AVENUE

CONTENTS

LIST OF ILLUSTRATIONS

[1] From *Cichorius*, "Reliefs der Trajanssaüle," Plate liv.
[2] From *Cichorius*, "Reliefs der Trajanssaüle," Plate xxxviii.
[3] From "Theodoric"; by kind permission of Dr. Hodgkin and of Messrs. Putnam's Sons.
[4] From "Julian, Philosopher and Emperor"; by kind permission of Messrs. Putnam's Sons.
[5] Kindly furnished by Mr. George Hill, of the British Museum.

PREFACE

———•◦•———

THIS book has been undertaken in consequence
of the friendly encouragement given to me by
several successful teachers of children, in schools
and at home, who seem to have thought well of my
previous attempt to make some historical persons
and incidents appeal to children's imagination. It
will be observed, however, that this is only in a very
general sense a sequel to my " Friends of the Olden
Time." In style it is adapted to the understanding
of young people who six or seven years ago may
have followed, without a feeling of outraged dignity,
our rambles and chats in the ancient world. The
biographical character of treatment has been partially
abandoned for the dramatic.

It may to some people seem absurd, yet I judge
it by no means impracticable, to lead even young
people to look at history as one great whole. In our
young days, as in the young days of history itself,
both ancient and mediæval, the unity of the whole

story of man was generally kept in view, a unity which gave it a kind of artistic grandeur and also caused it to abound in moral instruction. The unifying links were supplied from theories as to the Divine government of the World or the gradual upward progress of man. Now that we are more humbly reticent as to the ways of Providence, and perhaps less confident about the continuity of human progress, our historical views are apt to become fragmentary, and history loses its æsthetic interest without assuredly becoming more scientific. Perhaps it is only passing through a transition stage from which it will emerge as strong to impress the imagination, form the judgment, and brace the will, as ever it has been in the past.

For young learners of history, I believe it to be far the wiser plan to acquire first a strong impression, and an accurate knowledge of a few luminous patches in history, and to fill up gradually the duller spaces between, as time goes on. A few dates should be so fixed in the memory that they will remain there always, and afford, so to speak, large beads by help of which the length and the position of the intermediate parts of the chain may easily be reckoned.

I have endeavoured where possible to show the importance of monumental evidence as to facts and customs. Some of my illustrations have been chosen expressly with this view.

Finally, I would express my sincere gratitude to

all who have helped and encouraged me in my task,
and my earnest hope that they may find this little
work helpful to them. And if children ever read
prefaces—as, happily, they never do—I should give
my best thanks and most affectionate good wishes to
those who took my " Friends " as I meant them to
be taken, and to tell them that the thought that I
had given them some pleasure, and might help to
give them more, in what gives me more pleasure—
mixed with pain, as the best pleasures always are—
than anything else, had alone made it possible for me
to write this book.

ALICE GARDNER.

NEWNHAM COLLEGE, CAMBRIDGE,
            June, 1897.

SOME IMPORTANT EVENTS MENTIONED IN
THIS BOOK.

A.D.

20. Augustus recovers from the Parthians the Eagles lost by Crassus.

64. Great fire of Rome. Nero begins to persecute the Christians.

100. Trajan prepares for his war against the Dacians.

122. Hadrian in Britain.

235. Alexander Severus murdered by his soldiers.

330. Constantine founds Constantinople.

410. Alaric the Goth sacks Rome.

451. Attila the Hun beaten by Romans and Goths at Chalons.

500. Theodoric the Ostrogoth in Rome.

800. Charles the Great, King of the Franks, crowned Emperor in Rome.

1077. The Emperor Henry IV. does penance before Pope Gregory VII. at Canossa.

1300. Jubilee of Pope Boniface VIII.

1347. Rienzi Tribune in Rome.

1527. Rome sacked by the troops of the Emperor Charles V

ROME
THE MIDDLE OF THE WORLD

---◆◆◆---

CHAPTER I

INTRODUCTORY

HOW ROME BECAME THE MIDDLE OF THE WORLD

I AM writing this book chiefly for those who through me have made friends with *my* "Friends of the Olden Time." I feel that I have done for them the kind of service that a privileged lady may do for a young friend in presenting her at court. I dare say that a good many young people who have been presented never see the Queen again, yet I think that they are generally glad to have been near to her at least once in their lives, and she will seem a more really living person to them ever after. I hope, however, that some young people whom I have introduced to my "Friends" have had a good deal more than a hurried glance at their faces. I shall at least suppose that all who care to read this

book know, at any rate, as much about the Olden
Times as they could learn from the little visits we
made together. We are all older since that time,
and I hope we have all learned more, of history and
of other subjects, but I still keep to my principle,
that the best plan, if possible, for those who want
really to understand what was going on at any time
in the world's history, is to get hold of a man who
belongs to that time, and find out from him what he
thinks about things around him (though he may
often be utterly wrong), and—more important—to
see what he is *doing* to help or hinder the progress
or the changes going on. Of course this cannot
always be done: in some obscure periods few
persons stand out from among the rest so that we
can really know them, and either honour them or
shrink from them. Such periods may, nevertheless,
be very interesting, for nations and societies have
their characters and may be as attractive as private
persons. And besides, when you know much about
the character of a people and all its ways of life, you
may, by a little imagination, come to understand, or
at least to guess at, the kind of life and character
you would find in the men, women, and children
who make up that people, and so you feel almost as
if you knew them personally. But real personal
friendship is, where possible, the best introduction
to history, as into society generally.

Yet, though I keep to this notion as to the need
of friendship with men of the past for all those who

want to understand history, I am not going to try to make a book just like my other, only dealing with a later time. I intend to make two changes. For one thing, we are not going to rush about from period to period and country to country, seeking for interesting friends. We are older, and some of us less agile than we were, and for reasons which you may possibly see later on, it will be better for us to take our station at one place, which seems to be very much in the middle of all that is going on, and watch men and nations file past us, as, you will remember, King Xerxes sat on his throne looking towards the Ægean Sea, while all the mighty array of men from divers countries marched past him on their way (as he hoped) to conquer the Greeks. We shall be stationary as to place. But as to time, I shall, as before, make many leaps, and hurry over long periods, pointing out nothing but a guiding line. For I am not going to write for you a history of all the world, as seen from any one place during several centuries. That would be a heavy task, both for you and for me. But as the procession passes, I shall try to snatch a photograph of some one part of it, and we can study the picture at our leisure till another portion passes which is worth taking, though of course we must look at the Order of the Procession so as to know generally what has passed between the two parts that we have observed more closely.

Now this brings me to the second change I am

making in my way of bringing the past before you, or bringing you into the past. There are men in abundance belonging to the times we are to traverse who are well worth knowing, and who *can* be known. But while I desire you to interest your-selves in these men for their own sakes, I want you also to look at them with a larger interest, such as was impossible when you were yet children. It is a great step gained when you come to feel that men and women of old were in some ways so much like ourselves, in spite of such marked differences. The differences due to remoteness of time and place, to strangeness in language, in religion, in judgment as to right and wrong, come, after a time, to make historical personages all the more attractive to us, just as we enjoy meeting a Chinaman in his national costume or an Indian lady in her bright-coloured robes, and hearing from their lips of their own customs and thoughts, in some ways so like our own, in others so strangely unlike. But after we have overcome the feeling of strangeness, and have gained a personal feeling towards people of bygone times, we may go further and learn more from them by looking at them not only as our fellow-men and forerunners on life's path, but as *makers of history*.

For, in a sense, all history has been made by the men and women who have gone before us. I do not, of course, mean that any generation of men, or any particular set of men in any generation, decide in which way they would like the course of history to move, and then act accordingly. If the leading men at any time thus consciously and intentionally directed the progress of the world, history might still be a useful subject to study, but it would not be such a *great* subject as it is. I think we may safely say that though some great men see a few things, a little way off, very clearly, and go straight to the goal, yet many (and those of the very greatest) feel how little ahead they can see clearly, and so far from thinking of directing the course of the world, follow, and feel strongest when they follow, voices heard within or without which bid them do this or refrain from that and give no clear reason why. So that when we speak of men and nations *making* history, we think not of any great connected action planned and carried out by human effort. We think rather how each nation or society, and every man or woman in that society, has had some particular task to perform in bringing about a great result which the wisest of us can as yet see but dimly. We who care to study the past learn to appreciate the parts that men and groups or societies of men have severally contributed to the treasure which they have handed down to us. We often feel that we have suffered through their mistakes, that we have profited by their efforts and learned wisdom by their blunders ; we feel bitterly that they have wasted much that ought to have come down to us, and we regret also that we cannot impart to them the fruits of their own labours. "They, without us, might not be made

perfect," and likewise we cannot be made perfect, or fulfil our whole duty in life, except by
ministering to those who are to come after us.

As we watch the great march-past, then, we must
never be too sure that we know whence, at first,
it has come, nor whither it is going. But is it
possible to watch it at all ? Is there any point
from which we can see enough of it to make it
worth while to look at it at all ? For our present
purposes, and for the part of the procession we
want to watch, I answer without hesitating that
there *is* such a place, and that place is the City of
Rome.

But before we take up our position there, it is
as well to make quite sure why it is that we can
call Rome, during these times, the "Middle of the
World," and then how it is that she has come to
hold such an exalted position. Of course " Middle
of the World " is a figure of speech, and such
figures of speech are very apt to run away with us,
if we are not careful, and to make us talk nonsense.
We can hardly say that any place seems to us just
now the very centre of the World's life. To us
Englishmen, London may seem to come nearest to
that idea. Paris would seem the centre to all
Frenchmen. Americans would perhaps regard no
city in such a light. But all through the times
which we are to go into—first the time of the
Roman Empire and then that which, for reasons
that we may understand by and by, we call the

Middle Ages, there was no doubt in any one's mind that though one's own city might be nearer and dearer, yet none but Rome was *the* head-city of all the world. You know that it is not so now. Many people like to visit Rome so that they may see the ruins of her former greatness and the works of art that are stored in her museums. Others venerate the City as the residence of the Head of the Roman Catholic Church. But it would not make much difference to their lives and thoughts if they never realised that Rome was there. I am not speaking of Italians, of course. Rome is the seat of their government and the most important city of their country. But they do not regard her, and do not want to regard her, as belonging to other nations just as she belongs to them. And it is not quite easy to put into other words exactly what the many generations meant that called Rome the Head of the World. It did not exactly mean that she was the mistress that ruled over all countries and peoples, for the idea of her headship continued, as we shall see, long after she had lost her far-reaching political power. Nor yet did it mean that she was the most sacred of cities in the religious sense ; to Christians of the Middle Ages, Jerusalem seemed a holier city still. Nor was she in front of all other cities in learning and art. Athens and Alexandria were of greater reputation for those things than Rome had when Rome was at her best. But somehow, the course of historical events—that is, the

actions and sufferings of many generations which go
to make up history—had brought it about that Rome
found herself in a position such as no other city
has occupied before or after. She had come to be
regarded as the great protectress and diffuser of
what we call civilisation, though few of the people
who looked up to her would have put the idea into
those words. She was the centre of the Roman
Empire which was considered the *one* Empire, and
became the centre of the Western Church—which
regarded itself as the One Church. With other
empires and other churches we have nothing to do
just now. They did not look to Rome, yet we may
say, when we think how the world is now in a
sense bound in one, and how the most distant
lands depend for some things one on another, that
even they are different from what they would have
been if there had never been any Rome.

I have not exactly explained what we wanted to
explain, as to the meaning which we are to give to
the words " Rome the Middle of the World." But
there are a great many words that we can never
understand till we have industriously studied the
things that the words stand for. It is only by reading and thinking a good deal about the history of
Rome that you come to see the meaning of the names
that have been given her. Meantime, we may take
this practical meaning for ourselves—that when we
want to study the world in the times of the Emperors
and in the Middle Ages, we shall not miss the *most*

important events if we look first at what is going on in and about Rome. And the steps by which Rome has grown so great may be traced if you think over what you know of her history, *even* if (as I do not wish to believe) you know no more than what we gathered in our visits to my " Friends of the Olden Time."

We have paid an imaginary visit to Rome during the lifetime of grand old Camillus. That was in the year 367 B.C., just after the wars and perils Rome had undergone in the invasions of the Gauls, and just at the time when Rome was healing her own breach within the city, the conflict between Patricians and Plebeians. A compromise was being made, by which, among other things, it was to be arranged that of the Consuls, or chief magistrates of the State, *one* must always be a Plebeian. Now Rome had been founded, according to the date usually given, nearly four hundred years before this time, in the year 753 B.C. Of course we can know a good deal about Rome during these four hundred years, but I am sorry to say that very few of the legends of early Rome, which came, or used to come, at the beginning of all school histories, are to be taken as containing much sober fact. Almost all nations have legends about their earliest history, and their "brave days of old," just as we find numbers of stories told about the childhood of great men. But there are differences in these stories. Sometimes, in the case of great men, they arise from hazy memories of nurses and playmates, and in nations, from traditions proudly and lovingly handed down, and not losing anything in the process. Sometimes, the stories are made up long afterwards by people who think that the great man *ought* to have said and done wonderful things when he was a boy, or that the great nation *ought* to have heard prophecies of its future greatness, and to have been led by heroes worthy to be its first leaders. Now many, I fear most, of the stories of early Rome are of this second kind—they were made up afterwards, and therefore they are not worth much to us as history. But I would by no means go on to say that we ought not to know them, or that it is foolish to take pleasure in them. After all, we know the Romans, or any other people, much better for knowing what their own thoughts were about the people from whom they had sprung, and on what kind of stories the children were brought up, and how they got their first ideas of their duty to their country. Nevertheless, we must always be on the lookout, in reading history, to distinguish what is known to be true from what is only a doubtful story. And just at present I wish to keep within the boundaries of sober history.

To return, then, to the days of the great Camillus. Rome was so far, then, from being the middle of the world, that she was not even the greatest town of Italy. She was gradually gaining ground over the great cities of Northern Italy (you remember the story of the fall of Veii, the great Etruscan city), but there were still Greek colony-cities in the South of Italy beside which she might have seemed rude and barbarous. Many cities of her own neighbourhood, allied to her by kinship and by language and religious usages, were formed into a kind of league with her, and after a time, with some resistance on their part, and much actual fighting, these allied cities were obliged to give up some of their independence and look on Rome as their mistress. Roman power spread gradually in Italy. Whenever she had put down discontent anywhere, she built a fortress-city to keep the people in awe, and these cities were connected together by excellent roads, so that it became almost impossible to obtain back from her anything that she had once possessed. In time, every part of Italy, even the Greek cities that had once been so strong and great, were drawn into her net, and forced to make alliance with her on terms that practically made them her subjects.

Meanwhile, the old disputes between Patricians and Plebeians had come to an end. Fresh disputes and factions were to break out later on, but for some time Rome pursued her course, united and strong. After she had become the mistress of Italy, she was for a long while engaged in a life-and-death struggle with the great seafaring people of Carthage. What that struggle was like, and how it ended, you have already learned in making friends with Hannibal. You know, too, that after her wars with the Carthaginians, Rome obtained power over great countries beyond Italy, and forced them to pay tribute to her. We have seen also how Rome came to interfere in the affairs of Eastern lands, and how her interference ended in making her, not only judge between contending cities and princes, but mistress of all the civilised world (which means, roughly speaking, over all places where people talked and wrote in Greek or Latin), and of many barbarous peoples also. We have seen, too, that the wide conquests which Rome made were not altogether beneficial to her. The Italians were able to obtain corn from abroad at a very low rate, while the Roman people often had it given them for nothing, so that farming became as unprofitable a business to the small owners of corn-growing estates as it is to our tenant farmers in parts of England at the present day. Again, it was natural that when the State was constantly at war in distant parts, the great generals and their armies came to have more power than was desirable, and meantime the provinces were oppressed and plundered because the Senate could not or would not keep an eye on all that was going on, so as to know how Roman generals were acting in distant places. Thence came a series of seditions and agitations and at last civil wars. We have seen how the rumbling of the storm began with the Gracchi, and how the end of the Roman Republic came with the defeat and death of Cato the Stoic and the few who kept by him.

How is it, then, that Rome became the One Great

City of the World after she had seemed to sink under her burdens and calamities? The fact is, she had not died of her disease. She only needed a skilful physician to help her to recovery. Yet we know that when a person has had a bad illness, especially if he is no longer young, even after he has entirely recovered, he is not quite the same man that he was before. And so with some great cities and countries. Rome was like a man with a weak heart that has not vigour to pump the blood into the furthest capillaries of the long limbs. There came two great men in succession who by artificial means brought the centre and the extremities into closer connection. To drop figures of speech—which, as we have said, are apt to run away with us—it had become impossible for the Senate and People of Rome to control such a far-reaching empire. They could not have sufficed for the task when at their very best; and now the Senate was generally composed of a set of incapable and inert men of good family and of little else good, and the People was little better than a city mob. What was wanted was a master's eye, to watch with personal interest every part of the great machine, and one strong pair of hands to hold the threads by which the whole was bound together. Yet when Rome fell under the rule of *one* man, she lost what was good, though she may have gained what was better. She lost republican liberty, which is always an excellent thing for any people capable of using it aright. Some people, especially English and Americans, might think that when liberty is gone, nothing else remains worth having, but when we read Roman history, we feel that, sad as it was for Rome herself to lose her liberty, it was better for the world that she should not be allowed to keep it any longer.

Of the changes which gave Rome a new lease of life, and of the way in which they came about, I shall have more to say by and by. Just now I want you to realise that, in spite of quarrellings, and mistakes, and many failures, Rome really deserved to become the mistress of so many lands, and also that in a sense she was able to rise to the great occasion and to fulfil her duty to the world of which she had become the centre.

Rome deserved her position not only because she could fight better than her enemies, when it came to the actual conflict, but also because the Romans could patiently make sure of what they had conquered, could fortify, and make roads, and endure, if need be, great privations and hard labours. True, when you read about the wars of the Romans, you find cases of insubordination among the men and of blundering among the officers. But I think we may safely say that *no* army in ancient times was kept in discipline like that of the best modern armies; and the art of war had not yet been brought within the compass of rules such as those which all military officers are now obliged to learn. In orderly fighting and orderly governing, she was far ahead of peoples who were far beyond her in everything to do with art and literature and with the things that make life refined and easy. This is set forth in Macaulay's lay, "The Prophecy of Capys." In it he makes the Prophet address King Romulus :

> " Leave to the soft Campanian
>   His baths and his perfumes ;
> Leave to the sordid race of Tyre
>   Their dyeing-vats and looms ;
> Leave to the sons of Carthage
>   The rudder and the oar ;
> Leave to the Greek his marble Nymphs
>   And scrolls of wordy lore.
> Thine, Roman, is the pilum,
>   Roman, the sword is thine,
> The even trench, the bristling mound,
>   The legion's ordered line."

Those who read Virgil will some day come across, if they do not know it already, the very fine passage in the Roman poet which suggested these lines to Macaulay. It is as well to read also what was said by a man who was not a Roman, and so had no reason for boasting, and who wrote at a time (late in the second century B.C.) when Rome was already distracted by civic factions and seemed to be fast approaching the inevitable collapse :

" Now Judas (Maccabaeus) [1] had heard of the fame of the Romans, that they were mighty and valiant men, and such as would lovingly accept all that joined themselves unto them, and make a league of amity with all that came unto them ;

" And that they were men of great valour. It

---

[1] I Maccabees viii.

was told him also of their wars and noble acts which they had done among the Galatians, and how they had conquered them and brought them under tribute ;

" And what they had done in the country of Spain. . . .

" It was told him besides how they destroyed and brought under their dominion all other kingdoms and isles that at any time resisted them ;

" But with their friends and such as relied upon them they kept amity ; and that they had conquered kingdoms both far and nigh, insomuch as all that heard of their name were afraid of them ;

" Also that whom they would help to a kingdom, those reign ; and whom again they would, they displace : finally, that they were greatly exalted ;

" Yet for all this none of them wore a crown, or was clothed in purple, to be magnified thereby.

" Moreover have they had made for themselves a senate-house, wherein three hundred and twenty men sat in council daily, consulting alway for the people to the end they might be well ordered :

" And that they committed their government to one man every year, who ruled over all their country, and that all were obedient to that one, and that there was neither envy nor emulation among them " . . .

The man who wrote this was, you see, not quite well-informed as to facts. He did not know that there were *two* consuls in Rome, and he was, unfortunately, very far from the truth in supposing

that envy and emulation were unknown there ; but
the important thing to notice is that to those
accustomed to the kingdoms of the East which had
been founded as Alexander's empire fell to pieces,
the power, justice, and moderation of the Romans
seemed admirable in comparison.

But there is yet one more point to be noticed as
to the services which Rome did to the world at
large. We have seen that she became ruler over
peoples much superior to the Romans in power of
discerning and fashioning the beautiful, and of
searching after truth. And the Romans themselves
knew this, took the Greeks for their models, and
preserved, for us of a later day, a store of wealth in
the Greek books which they copied and preserved,
and in the statues which they kept or imitated.
True, they did not always discern between the
excellent and the second-rate. They sometimes
showed their appreciation of beautiful statues by
stealing them away from their proper places to
adorn their own houses and gardens, and when they
copied the Greek style of writing books, they fell
very far short of their masters. Still, Rome became
a place where learned and clever men met and
thought and wrote, and where artists laboured for
rich employers. Knowledge and skill of all kinds,
luxury and refinement, all that Egypt, and Greece,
and Phœnicia, and even distant India had excelled
and delighted in, might in some form be found in
the city which had obtained dominion by her

military power and kept it by her capacity of ordering and ruling.

Perhaps we can now see how Rome was at one time the Middle of the World. But how she continued to be the middle for many hundreds of years, we can only understand after following her later fortunes.

AUGUSTUS.

.

CHAPTER II

AUGUSTUS, AND WHAT HE DID FOR ROME

IF ever you go to the Vatican Museum in Rome, you will see a statue, at which, when it has once caught your eye, you must needs look again and again.

It is a more-than-life-size figure of a warrior, clad in a short Roman tunic, with a magnificent breast-plate over it, and a cloak which seems to have fallen about his waist. His right hand is stretched out, as if he were addressing his army ; in his left he holds a spear.[1] Close to his right foot nestles a little Cupid, with a dolphin. His features are those of a man under middle-life, and are wonderfully clear-cut and faultless. His hair, cut short, hangs a little over his forehead, and he has no beard. On the breastplate certain figures are skilfully embossed. In the middle you see a Roman soldier, with a dog, or perhaps a wolf (an ancestress of whom, you know, suckled Romulus and Remus), and before him stands

---

[1] It has been restored as a sceptre, but was probably a spear

a barbarian, handing over to him a Roman standard. Above them the Sun-god drives his chariot. Everything about the man—the calm dignity of his face, his commanding attitude, the glorious story figured on his breastplate, seems suggestive of the majesty of the Roman name. And this is right and fitting, for the man is no other than Augustus, the first Emperor of Rome.

We have another memorial of him, sculptured by men of his own time, and preserved for our neverceasing admiration—all his great deeds recorded by himself. These were engraved in stone, and a clear copy of them was placed round the walls of a temple to Rome and to Augustus at Ancyra in Asia Minor. "A temple to himself ?" you ask. "Surely he did not make himself a god, nor the City of Rome a goddess !" Not exactly, perhaps. People worshipped the genius of Cæsar and the fortune of Rome, and it was not till the Emperor was dead that he was . regarded as being actually one of the gods. But probably those who shared in these worships were not quite clear as to whom or what they were worshipping. One thing was certain : they acknowledged the power of the Roman Empire to be as worthy of their adoration as was that of the Immortal Gods.

But to return to the inscription : it was probably meant to stand round the Emperor's tomb—to serve, in fact, as his epitaph, but copies of it were made for several temples. It is an autobiography, from his nineteenth to his sixty-seventh year, and is composed both in Latin and in Greek. Epitaphs do not always tell us the *whole* truth about those who lie below. In this case, however, though certain unpleasant memories are passed over, what is recorded is stated very simply, and is almost all confirmed by the historians who have written of the time. In fact, the record is so great that it needs no great flourish of trumpets or of words to make its real greatness appear. Still, a little-minded man might not have seen that. In simple, business-like language, the Emperor tells of the various titles, honours, and offices that, at various times, the Senate and People of Rome have conferred upon him, the victories that he has gained, and the triumphs he has celebrated. As simply, and perhaps more proudly, he tells of the triumphs he has refused to celebrate and the offices he has declined to hold. He tells how he liberated the Roman State from the dread of insurgents at home and foes abroad ; how he brought about universal peace, and thrice caused the Temple of Janus (which, as you of course know, was always open in times of war) to be closed ; how he gave shows to the people, remitted grievous taxes from distressed districts, settled flourishing colonies in Italy itself and in various parts of Europe, Africa, and Asia, built temples and market-halls ; how, when at last the need for his extraordinary powers was over, he gave back to the Senate and People the sovereignty

they had entrusted to him in their day of need.
And all this, though (especially with this last statement about sovereign power) we have sometimes
to read between the lines, is acknowledged on the
authority of his contemporaries to be simple matter
of fact.

He was one of the most successful men that ever
lived, and when we look at the vast work that he
accomplished, we are obliged to call him a great
man.   Yet his name has not come down the stream
of history among those of the men for whom we
feel a living gratitude and affection.   If his uncle,
Julius Cæsar, were to walk into a modern hall, full
of learned men, some might shrink from him, but
many would rush to grasp him by the hand, and
many more would form an admiring circle round
him.   But if Augustus were to come in, all would
look at him with interest and wonder, and some
might give up their chairs to him—but I doubt
whether any would wish to embrace him.   The
fact is, he has always been a puzzle to all historians.   Some of his deeds, especially in his early
youth, appear treacherous and cruel in a high
degree.   Yet in this " Monument " he rejoices to
record how many people he has spared, and how
he has given refuge to fugitive princes, and made
the Roman name honoured.   He was cautious in
his youth, cautious to the very end, all are agreed
on that point.   He was able to feel strong affection, but when the objects of his affection had gone

astray, they never found him ready to forgive.   Yet if we are disgusted at his youthful heartlessness, if we feel repelled by his cool craftiness, and if even our pity for his home troubles is lessened by a suspicion that he kept down his family, or certainly his daughter, with too tight a hand, let us remember that to him must be accorded the merit of living and thinking always for his country, and of giving it prosperity and peace.

But let us look now at his earlier and not altogether creditable, though very successful career, and see how it brought him into a position of such lofty power.

Every one who has read Shakespeare's "Julius Cæsar" and "Antony and Cleopatra" (that is, of course, among Englishmen, everybody who has read anything at all worth reading) knows something about the difficulties of Octavian's early life.   We call him *Octavian* (before he received the title of Augustus), because, when he was adopted by his great-uncle, Julius Cæsar, he dropped the name of *Octavius*, inherited from his father, and became known as Gaius Julius Cæsar Octavianus.   In fact— and this is a point which, if you ever want to feel at home among the Romans, you must always bear in mind—*adoption* meant a great deal more among the Romans than it ever does to us, and an adopted son used to speak of the man who had adopted him as *my father*, and to think of him as a father, without, at the same time, losing all sense of kinship with his own blood-relations. Octavian, then, had been educated under Cæsar's eye, and by Cæsar's will he was acknowledged as his son and heir. After Cæsar had been murdered, on the Ides of March, 44 B.C., young Octavian came to Rome, and found a state of parties and affairs there among which it would have been hard for the cleverest and most experienced statesman to steer his way. The chief of the murderers, Brutus and Cassius, had been allowed to go abroad, but many of the leading men in Rome sympathised with them. Mark Antony, the friend of Cæsar, who by his oration over the dead body of Cæsar had moved the Romans to rage against the slayers and veneration for the slain, was a very important person in Rome, and Octavian was obliged to pay some regard to him. At the same time, he had to consider the Senators, among whom Cicero's eloquence was just now very powerful, and who were becoming much irritated by Mark Antony's masterful ways. But the young man showed himself more than a match for all those with whom he had to deal. He insisted on Antony's giving up to him those of Cæsar's papers and sums of money which he was keeping in his own hands. Soon after, when the Senate proclaimed Antony a public enemy, Octavian obtained the chief command against him. He had already won over to his interests large bodies of the soldiers, who loved the name of Cæsar. Antony was beaten, but the two consuls who, with Octavian, had been sent against

him were killed. Octavian came suddenly back to
Rome, that he might receive the honour of Consul
for himself. Then, instead of pursuing Antony, he
without delay came to terms with him. The two,
with an eminent general Lepidus, met together near
Bologna in North Italy and agreed on a plan by
which they should share among themselves all the
honour and the power of the State, and cause their
enemies to be put to death. The powerless Senate
could not but submit to this Triumvirate, or Three-
men-rule, and Rome lost many good citizens by the
" Proscriptions" which are the greatest blot on the
memory of Octavian.

Then Brutus and Cassius had to be put down.
The battle of Philippi ended the resistance and the
lives of them both. As might be expected, the
Triumvirs did not long act together in harmony.
Antony fell under the influence of Cleopatra, queen
of Egypt, and his life and rule became like that of a
sultan rather than like that of a Roman magistrate.
Octavian tried his best to recall him to his promises
and his duty, but in vain. Lepidus, too, showed
signs of discontent, but he was not a very active
man, and was soon brought down to a more modest
position. Meantime Sextus Pompeius, son of the
great Pompey, had been making himself so powerful
by sea that the triumvirs were for a short time
obliged to make an agreement with him, but war
broke out again, and Pompey was defeated and put
to death. Finally, the Senate declared war against

Antony and Cleopatra. Octavian sailed against them. The battle was fought off the promontory of Actium on the west coast of Greece. Cleopatra sailed off in a fright, Antony followed her. The death of both within a short time put an end to the war, and left all the Roman world, with Egypt added, at the feet of Octavian, who now occupied a position even more exalted than that of his uncle after the defeat and death of Pompey.

In his "Monument" Augustus tells this story briefly and truly, but omitting some of the puzzling details: "When I was nineteen years old, I raised an army by my own counsel and at my own expense, and thus I restored liberty to the State, which lay bound under the power of one party. . . . Those who had killed my father, I sent into exile, and by means of a lawful decree I avenged their crime ; and afterwards, when they took up arms against the Republic, I defeated them in two battles. I took the command in wars by land and by sea, at home and abroad, all over the world, and when I had conquered, I pardoned the citizens that remained. So far as it was safe I preferred to spare foreign nations also rather than to destroy them." Yet these are the words of the man to whose influence the " Proscription " and the horrible murders which followed were chiefly due ! Perhaps he thought afterwards of this piece of work as part of the "avenging of his father." But many men who were put to death with his consent—Cicero for example—were as innocent of

Cæsar's murder as he was himself. Some historians think that his desire to avoid bloodshed and to show mercy was a growth of later years, as the feeling of power made him realise the duties of a great governor. Be this as it may, Octavian rose, whether by fair means or by foul, in any case by means of his own genius, to the head of the Roman world, and once there, he could afford to be merciful, and found his chief good in ministering to the well-being of his people, or, as he might have put it, to the good of the Republic, and of the whole world.

This task meant many warlike and many peaceful undertakings. He tells us that he cleared the sea of pirates, and that was indeed a service to the Empire, of which all the parts were bound together in ever-active trade. In some directions, as he said, he extended the limits of the Provinces. In the far East, he gained, without actual warfare, what he evidently regarded as his greatest triumph. During the time when Cæsar and Pompey were acting together, an army was given to the wealthy Roman Crassus, who was friendly to them both, that he might chastise the Parthians. At Carrhæ, between the Euphrates and the Tigris, a terrible battle was fought. Crassus and his son were killed, the Roman standards lost, and the splendid army destroyed. The head of Crassus was taken to the barbarous king, and when, in a play that was being acted before him, a wild woman was to enter bearing the head of her slaughtered son, it was thought a fine thing to have a *real* head, that of a Roman general, to serve the purpose. Julius Cæsar had since fought against the Parthians and worsted them, but he had never got the standards back. Augustus, however, without marching against the Parthians, but after arranging the succession to the neighbouring kingdoms of Armenia and of Media, and showing himself in Syria, received a humble embassy from King Phraates, with three of the lost eagles, which he placed in the Temple of Mars the Avenger. Many medals were struck, and congratulatory poems were written on this occasion, and it surely deserved them all, for it marked the awe-striking power of the Roman Name.

In another quarter, Augustus, or generals sent by him, waged great wars—among the Germans on the northern frontier, men who were to become very terrible to Rome in later days. One great disaster occurred, which Augustus did not commemorate on his "Monument," though he felt the importance of it keenly enough. The Roman general Varus was marching against a confederacy of German tribes, that the Emperor's stepsons had endeavoured to make subject. But the German hero Arminius and his hosts fell on the legions while they wandered in the woods, and put them to a terrible slaughter. Varus felt his incompetency and slew himself. This happened soon before the death of Augustus, *where* we cannot be quite certain, but probably near Osnabrück, where our King George I.

died. As I said, Augustus was not among those men whose pride can never recognise failure. In bitterness of soul he cried aloud, " Varus, give me back my legions." And he sent his stepson to repair the defeat, if possible. But though one of the eagles lost in the Teutoberger Forest was afterwards recovered, yet the memory of the defeat remained.

Before he died, Augustus left a piece of wise advice to his successor : not to try to increase the Empire. He saw that if it reached from the Atlantic Ocean to the Euphrates, and from the deserts of Arabia to the Rhine, it was quite big enough. His successors, as a rule, kept to his advice ; not entirely—or Britain would never have been conquered. But, generally, the wiser among the Emperors cared more about guarding the frontier than of extending it. This frontier-guarding was always an important matter for the Empire, and you would do well to study it if you want to know how the Empire stood so long and why it broke down at last.

I have spoken about *Augustus* and about the *Emperors*, but have not yet said what those words actually meant. The term *Imperator* was at first equal to " triumphant general," and was often bestowed on the field of battle by the acclamations of the soldiers. Twenty-one times in his life Augustus was saluted as *Imperator* in this sense. But the *imperial* power given him by law, and denoted by the title *Imperator* placed *before* his

name, was something more really important than
this, and carried with it supreme military command
in all parts of the Empire. As to *Augustus*, that
was a complimentary title, decreed to him when
he did what we have seen he described as giving
back the State to the management of the Senate
and People. In point of fact, he did no such
thing, and it would not have been wise of him to
do it. The Senate and People were not at that
time fit to govern the State. What he really meant
to do was to declare that he did not wish to be
consul for life, nor censor for life, nor to keep his
old powers as *Triumvir*. He was willing enough to
keep some exceptional powers. For one thing,
he received and kept the power of the Tribunes.
You remember how that magistracy was first
instituted for the protection of the poor and low-
born against the wealthy and noble, and how the
complete equalisation of Patricians and Plebeians
took away all its meaning and character, till something of its old spirit was given back to it by the
Gracchi. Another and a yet stranger alteration
comes when it is used by a man who is to all
intents and purposes a monarch, to veil his supreme
authority. But at all times the Tribunes of the
Plebs had held some remarkable powers, and their
persons were held sacred, so that the great Emperor
did not think it below his dignity to make much of
the tribunician power which had been granted to
him. One of his chief titles was *Princeps*, or head

man in the State.   I need hardly say that he would
never have called himself *King*.   The People would
not have endured it, and, after all, the tastes of
Augustus were not those of a rich Oriental despot.
He liked to wear the clothing that his wife and
daughters had woven for him.   He did not wish
to shut himself off from the world, but preferred
to figure as the first citizen of a free State.   And
though the State was not really free, yet he felt
towards the institutions of his country as he says
he felt towards conquered nations : he preferred to
spare them whenever it was safe.   To this end,
he divided with the Senate the care of providing
governors for the Provinces.   Those Provinces
which were in a settled and peaceful state were
called Senatorial, and were under the government
of proconsuls and proprætors sent by the Senate.
Those not yet thoroughly conquered, or frequently
requiring the presence of an army, were the special
care of the Emperor himself and his legates.   But
even in the senatorial Provinces there were some
officials directly responsible to the Emperor himself,
so that the " master's eye " overlooked the whole
provincial system as it had never been overlooked
before.

In his home life the successful Emperor was
anything but happy.   He had one daughter, Julia,
whom he loved dearly, but who showed herself
so unworthy of his affection that he was obliged
to disown her and to mourn her loss more than if

she were dead. Of her four children he adopted
the two elder, attended carefully to their education,
and bestowed honours on them which they were
too young to deserve. But both died within two
years, while scarcely more than youths, and of
Julia's younger children, a boy and a girl, one was
insane and the other wicked. The second wife of
Augustus, Livia, had been married already, and her
sons grew up in the Emperor's household and held
important commands in the army. But the abler
of the two died early, and the other, Tiberius, who
succeeded Augustus, lived a sad and discontented
life. To his wife, Livia, Augustus was tenderly
attached. We know, from busts and medals, that
she was beautiful. She *may* have been good likewise, but the scandalmongers, whose unkind gossip
often goes down as history, were very busy about
her good name.

There was another matter, besides the Proscriptions, the defeat of Varus, and domestic troubles,
which Augustus did not mention on his " Monument," simply because he knew nothing about it,
though for the world in general it was far the
most important event of his time.

" It came to pass . . . that there went out a
decree from Cæsar Augustus that all the world
should be taxed, and . . . ," you know the rest of
the story. I need not say here anything about the
birth and its importance, except this : that the
more one reads about the Roman Empire, the more

one realises how much fairer a field the message of the Apostles had than it would have had if the story they had to tell had happened a little earlier. The Roman Peace had for a time given a kind of unity to all nations, and removed barriers which might have hampered the progress of the new teaching. We shall hear of persecutions by and by, but at first we find that Christian teachers, even if they excite popular prejudice, are protected—not without a grain of contempt—by the Emperors and by their authority.

One biographer of Augustus says that when he was on his death-bed, he asked his friends whether he had played his part in life well, and on their answering " yes," went on : " Then clap me." Posterity has clapped him, without always realising what was the post which he filled so ably. Perhaps we cannot feel sure exactly what he meant. Did he mean to say that all his life had been pretence and not reality ; that, for instance, when he professed to give back liberty to the State, he was laughing in his sleeve at the senators ? Or did he want to say that, at that supreme moment, all human life seemed to him a vain show, and that there is no reality about it worth looking for ? Or did he mean that life, whatever we think of it, is beyond our comprehension, and that the ablest man is but the actor in a piece which he has not written and cannot know except as to his own part ? Whatever he meant, we may take his words in this

last sense, and applaud his acting in so far as it led
to the establishment of peace and unity, and the
settling of Rome in her position as the "Middle
of the World."   .

The success and the glory of the reign are, of
course, not due to Augustus only. If, as he said,
he found a city of brick and left one of marble, his
friend Agrippa, to whom Rome owes her wonderful
Pantheon, was almost as great a builder as the
Emperor. If great writers—Virgil, Horace, Livy—
enjoyed peace and leisure in his day, it was his
minister, Mæcenas, who was the most famous
friend and patron of learned men. Yet Augustus
cared much for learning, art, and all things that
could make the city glorious. We render him due
honour when we give, both to his own time and
to any other time as renowned as his in literature
and art, the title of *Augustan Age*.

CHAPTER III

NERO AND HIS TIMES

IF a young man had left Rome at the time of the death of Augustus, buried himself in complete solitude, and then returned to the great city, he would naturally, as he approached it, wonder how far he should find things as he had left them. Would the successors of Augustus have had the wisdom and the strength to carry on his work and to maintain that strange form of government which had been begun by him, a government in which the powerful head of the State seemed to share his authority with a Senate that looked very venerable and did very little work, and a People that looked like a rabble and did nothing but lounge and sometimes quarrel? The emperors would probably have done something to make the city itself more dignified and beautiful, and more convenient of access. On this point our traveller, if he approached from the sea, would soon find his conjectures right, as he admired the new and spacious harbour. Would they have succeeded in maintaining the impressive power as well as the imposing appearance of the Head of the World? Would the people of Italy and of the Provinces have been kept in obedience and good order? Would the threatening barbarians have been kept in check, and would the State have been kept free from serious civil strife? And as he passed on, eager to compare the Rome to which he was returning with the Rome of fifty years before, the question uppermost in his mind would be: If the successors of Augustus still bear rule, what manner of man is he who holds Augustus' seat to-day?

He would be likely to think, as historians of that day and of later days have thought, that the answer to this question was all-important. But after all, we are generally likely to overrate the influence that one man can exercise, however great his authority, over a vast extent of country, the government and the general customs of which have been for some length of time going along pretty much the same ways. There are certain times at which the thoughts of one man's mind and the force of one man's will may do much to mould the form of history for many years afterwards, though in no case will that form be entirely of his own design. But in ordinary times, customs, and fixed ways of thinking and of acting, and the character of people of different nations and classes, make things go on in a line on which they have been started, so that the freaks of one driver need not, so to speak, upset the whole coach. It was very important for the world that Augustus came when he did, and it was important, likewise, that his successor should be a man of ability, capable of following in his footsteps. Yet we find that the fourth emperor after Augustus was a man whose name has been a byword for extravagant wickedness, and that in spite of him, Rome shows no sign of ceasing to be the centre of all things. The historians naturally tell us a good deal about the court and the evil deeds of the Emperor and of those who surrounded him in his later years, and thus they sometimes lead us to think that the Empire as a whole was in a worse plight than it really was. But often the folly and wickedness of a court are like the smoky atmosphere of a big modern town, which only infects those within a narrow circle, and lets the country around remain sweet and wholesome. If we look a little while at the reign of this most hated and dreaded of emperors, we shall see how even during that time the majesty of Rome remained as grand as ever, and how, even through some of the Emperor's own dark deeds, Rome came to be looked on as the Middle of the World by a new set of people whose way of regarding her came to be more important later on.

Nero—for he is the Emperor of whom I am speaking—was, as just said, the most hated of emperors : at any rate, after he had grown to what should have been years of discretion. Yet his character is in some ways attractive, just as some singularly ugly persons have a kind of charm about them that *plain* people never have. He is generally reckoned as the last emperor of the line of Augustus. The relations of the emperors are rather complicated, owing to the Roman practice of *adoption* which I have already mentioned, and also to the inter-marriages within the Imperial family. Nero was a direct descendant of Augustus, because his mother, Agrippina, was daughter of another Agrippina, whose mother was Julia, daughter of Augustus, of whose sad and disgraceful history we have already spoken. At the same time, Nero's grandfather, husband of the elder Agrippina, was the son of an adopted son of Augustus, real son of his wife Livia. But his descent alone would not have brought him to the head of the State, especially as the reigning Emperor, his great-uncle Claudius, had a young son of his own. All his greatness he owed to his mother Agrippina. She was a most ambitious and beautiful woman, desperately wicked, if we are to believe even the milder of the stories told against her, but apparently devoted to the interests of her child. There was a story told that on the birth of Nero (or Lucius Domitius, as his name ran at first), a star-gazer foretold that this child should reign, and that he should murder his mother; and that when this was repeated to Agrippina, she cried out, " Let him murder me if only he reigns." She made his way and her own by obtaining first her marriage

with the Emperor, although he was her own uncle,
and then the adoption of her boy by her new
husband. Soon after, she obtained the young
daughter of Claudius, Octavia, as Nero's bride.
And when, in the year 54, the dull, unhappy, but
not altogether foolish Emperor died—poisoned, it
was said, by the wicked wiles of his wife—she kept
the matter secret till preparations had been made
for proclaiming young Nero Emperor.

This was done partly by means of the Imperial
Guards, whom she had gained to her side, partly by
the consent of the poor-spirited Senate, which, though
there must still have been some good men in it, had
lost every shred of its ancient dignity. Besides this,
Claudius had not been much beloved, and Nero began
his reign by making fair promises of justice, moderation, and good government, some of which were
kept for several years. In the earlier days of Nero
he was guided chiefly by two men, Burrhus, captain
of the Guards, and the philosopher Seneca. This
man is a very interesting person in Nero's court.
He was a Stoic philosopher, and came from Spain
—for at this time the great men of the Spanish cities
considered themselves just as much Romans as if
they had been born in sight of the Capitol. We
have seen in the story of Cato of Utica how the
doctrines of the Stoics—the doctrines which taught
men to despise luxury, to practise self-control, and
to follow duty in spite of pains and threatenings—
had laid hold of some of the best of the Romans

and had even yielded fruit in their lives. Now Seneca seems to have been sincere in his Stoicism as far as it went, but during part of his life he had laboured more to put it into elegant words than into strong deeds, and I confess that in his treatises written to comfort himself and others in the troubles that befell them, his words seem to me to lack the ring of reality. However, he had good ideas—especially he had grasped the notion that all mankind form one body or brotherhood, and that thus we ought all to work together, in mutual help and forbearance. Now, when he was made tutor to Nero—who was still a mere boy, and who seemed as yet a promising and clever one—he had to write the Emperor's speeches for him, and to give advice in appointing officers and making decrees. On such occasions he felt that he had scope for putting his ideas into practice on a grand scale. Unfortunately he found it very hard to keep to his practical Stoicism amid the luxury and want of principle all around him. The court, the corruption of the State, the dangerous disposition of Nero himself, proved too strong for him. There was such a great temptation to make little of Nero's evil deeds in order to keep the power that might restrain him from worse. Perhaps he yielded to worse temptations and encouraged Nero to take up frivolous pursuits in order that he might not interfere in business. But Seneca had enemies about court, and we cannot be certain as to the truth of what was alleged against him, nor as to the length he went in encouraging Nero's wickedness. His death, like that of Cranmer, or of Charles I., may reflect a light of honour on a less honourable life. He was accused of conspiring against the Emperor and ordered to kill himself. With great fortitude, after comforting his servants and his faithful wife, who desired to share his fate, he opened his veins and continued his exhortations to those around him while life lasted. His was one of the many lives of distinguished men that became victims to Nero's ferocity in his later years.

The first black deed which stands against Nero's name is the murder of his cousin Britannicus, son of the Emperor Claudius, whom he caused to take poison in a cup of wine-and-water. The sister of this boy, Octavia, had, as we have said, been already married to Nero, but she was not to his taste, and he wished to marry another lady. This was one of the causes of disagreement between Nero and his mother. At first, Nero seemed to appreciate what Agrippina had done for him. He gave to his guard, the night after the death of Claudius, for watchword, " Best of mothers." But Agrippina expected more than gratitude and affection from him. She insisted on taking part in all public business, sitting in the Senate, and helping to receive ambassadors. Seneca and Burrhus regarded this behaviour as against all rules of decency. The Romans reverenced their women—Seneca had a mother who could enter into his philosophy—but they objected to anything like female government. Perhaps Nero shared their views; certainly he was vexed that she took the part of Octavia and would not leave him alone. For some time mother and son were estranged from one another; then Nero planned a meeting which was supposed to be with a view to reconciliation. He invited her to a gorgeous supper in a villa of his near the seashore. She came, was magnificently entertained, and was provided, by the thoughtful generosity of her son, with a beautifully arranged boat for her return journey. As they went along smoothly in the star-lit night, the part of the boat containing the Empress's apartment seemed to be coming to pieces. One of her servants, made deceitful through cowardice, rushed out, shouting, "I am the Empress, save me!" Her reward was a blow from an oar which struck her dead. Agrippina suspected foul play, but being a vigorous woman in body as in mind, succeeded, by swimming and by floating on pieces of the boat, in escaping to shore. Arrived at home, she sent an ironical message to Nero, telling him of her happy deliverance. As she awaited the answer in a dimly-lit chamber, messengers from Nero arrived, who struck her down and killed her then and there. The Senate was quite ready to receive Nero's apology, that his mother had been plotting against him. Octavia was banished to an island, and her head was cut off and taken to the lady who had become Nero's second wife.

The years that follow were the worst of Nero's reign. Many innocent people were put to death because the Emperor suspected or disliked them, and money was taken on all manner of excuses to provide for Nero's costly banquets and extravagant humours.

Now these fancies of Nero's were some of them like those we read of in other young princes who make their rank an excuse for wild freaks and nightly follies, like those of our own Prince Hal— only much worse. But others were peculiar to himself. In spite of all his faults, Nero cared for what is beautiful in art, for poetry and music and plays, and like many people who wish to be thought clever in anything that is *not* their proper business, he desired above all things to be, and to be known to be, a good player on the lyre, an actor and composer of plays, and even a skilful charioteer. He instituted a new festival, the Neronia, and performed himself, at first privately in his own gardens, afterwards publicly before a large audience. Of course he was always applauded and received all the prizes, whether he did well or ill. The old Romans had always felt contempt for those that performed in public—they would not have tolerated our amateur theatricals and charity concerts ; and to any who dared to think—hardly any one dared to speak—it seemed a most shocking

thing that Nero should not only behave in this out-
rageous way himself, but induce Romans of good old
families to do the like. Yet Nero's tastes were artistic,
not altogether low. He does not seem to have cared
much for the hateful gladiatorial shows in which the
people of his time took so much delight. He was
cruel in his punishments sometimes, but in games
and amusements he was not generally brutal, though
frivolous and unreasonable in the extreme. He had
a great respect for everything Greek, or everything
that seemed to him Greek in character, and he once
made a journey to Greece and ordered that the
great games, which used, of course, to be celebrated
at regular intervals, sometimes of four years, should
this time be celebrated all in one year, that he might
compete in each. He built a large mansion for
himself within the sacred enclosure at Olympia,
which must have contrasted strangely with the
simple, majestic temples reared in nobler days. It
is needless to say that Nero was declared victor in
every contest for which he entered himself. The
way in which he respected the Greeks, in spite of
the liberties he took with their institutions, is shown
in a meeting which he held at Corinth, that he
might express his goodwill to the people, and
promise them what he called liberty, with remis-
sion of the tribute formerly paid. For even Nero
felt the influence which the land of the Greeks and
the remembrance of her great men of old has always
cast over those who realise that in many things no

nation, certainly not the Roman, nor yet the English, will ever attain to the measure of the Greeks *at their best*. And though it would seem almost sacrilegious to compare a depraved ruffian like Nero with a hero like Alexander, yet they are alike in one or two respects : in their ardent and extravagant admiration for Greek arts and Greek life, and again in their occasional bursts of uncontrolled rage, which in both cases seems a kind of madness bred by the possession of unlimited, irresponsible power. But Alexander was a man of strong will and never-failing courage, a real man indeed. Nero was a dilettante, and in the end proved to be a coward. For one practical and sensible notion, however, we must here give him credit. He saw what a good thing it would be for the trade between East and West if a canal were dug through the Isthmus of Corinth, and ordered the work to be done. But it was not finished, and only in our own days has the scheme been carried out.

About two years before Nero's visit to Greece, there occurred a calamity at Rome of terrible magnitude. A fire broke out in a very populous part of the city, which raged for five days, and left many people homeless. It also destroyed many of the most ancient buildings of Rome, especially the temple of Jupiter Stator, said to have been built by Romulus. Nero was not in Rome at the time, but he returned speedily, opened his private gardens to the homeless people, and did all he could to relieve the distress. The fire was stopped at last by the same means used in London at the great fire of 1667—houses were pulled down and gaps left, so that the rushing flames might have nothing left to feed upon. The part destroyed was rebuilt in much grander style. It is an odd thing for us, with our notions as to sanitary streets and buildings, to read that some people thought the new wide streets unhealthy, because they afforded so little shelter from the sun. Nero himself took advantage of the empty space to build himself a magnificent palace, with porticoes of polished marble, luxurious banqueting-halls, and artificially laid-out gardens, including a kind of zoological gardens of strange beasts. Now those who hated Nero said that he had caused the fire himself, and that as he looked on it, he sang to the lyre the story of the burning of Troy. This latter story might not seem impossible in the case of one so fond of acting and of impressive situations as he was ; but it does not bear out the charge of firing the city, which seems almost incredible, though one historian says that Nero had a great appetite for the incredible. However, the fact that some in Rome did suspect him seems to have led Nero to follow up the charges made against another set of people of whom we now hear for the first time in the writings of the historians—the Christians.

It seems strange to us that so monstrous a charge should have been made. But we must remember that as yet the Christians were little thought of by

the upper classes, and the lower classes believed all
manner of evil against them, such as that they ate
babies at their solemn meetings, and committed all
manner of crimes. In fact, the curious charges
brought against them are much like those that the
Chinese have brought against English and French
missionaries in our days. They were not, however,
much persecuted. The Roman government allowed
all the people in the Empire to worship according
to their ancestral rites; but the Christians did not
belong to any of the old, "respectable" religions,
which men followed as their fathers had done before
them. There were laws by which people who met
secretly for purposes that might bring evil to society
generally might be punished. Still, as yet, till this
year 64 A.D., the Christian assemblies had not fallen
under grave suspicion among people who were
fairly reasonable and understood the laws. The
Christians were mostly poor people, often slaves.
St. Paul remarked to the Corinthians, probably
about this time : " Not many wise men after the
flesh, not many mighty, not many noble are called."
The historian Tacitus felt bound to find out something about them, and discovered, as he said, that
they derived their name from one called Christ, who
had been put to death in the reign of Tiberius, by
the Procurator, Pontius Pilate; and that their
detestable superstition, which had begun in Judæa,
had even spread to the Great City, where all things
foul naturally sought a home. Furthermore, he

says that on this occasion they were accused and
convicted not so much of the burning, as of being
"haters of the human race." This last phrase may
sound strange to us, but rightly understood it would
probably explain the frenzy of the people against
the Christians which brought about this first persecution. These converts (there was hardly time for
any to have been brought up as Christians) had no
sympathy with the pagan society in which they
lived. They could not join in any festivities of the
family or the nation, for all were mixed with idola-
trous rites. They cared to perform no more of their
civil duties than was necessary, for they regarded
the old world as doomed, and looked "for a new
heaven and a new earth, wherein dwelleth righteousness." No wonder people disliked and misunder-
stood them. If Tacitus had taken the pains to ask
any of them about their beliefs, they might have
told him what would have interested him. But he
naturally thought such questioning not worth the
trouble. Nor should we blame him, nor yet, beyond
a certain degree, the people who looked on the first
Christians with disgust. If any of our friends were
to cease to come to our parties, and especially our
Christmas jollity; to keep away from christenings,
weddings, and funerals, to profess no interest in
politics or in any of the interests of the day, we
should probably set them down as surly and dis-
agreeable people—and we might possibly judge them
as unfairly as the Roman people judged the Chris-

tians.   But the cruelties which followed the popular
rage, and especially the part that Nero took in them,
cannot be regarded as capable of any sort of excuse.
Some of the Christians were dressed in skins of wild
beasts, and set to fight with real wild beasts for the
amusement of the people. Others perished by fire in
such fashion that their burning limbs might help to
lighten up Nero's gardens for a chariot race.   Yet
to after generations the sufferings they endured
seem as nothing in comparison with the crown of
martyrdom which Nero's government bestowed
upon them.   Rome was not only a powerful, she
had become a sacred city, in that she held the tombs
of the earliest martyrs.   Tradition soon increased
that reverence tenfold, since the story came to be
universally believed that both St. Peter and St. Paul
had suffered death for their faith at about this time.
Now the historic truth of this statement may be
doubted, but the fact that it was believed became
of great importance in the future.   For some
hundreds of years if you had asked any ordinary
person, " Why is Rome the Middle of the World ? "
he would not have thought of her ancient conquests,
nor of Augustus, nor even of the great fortress and
great temples and mansions in Rome, but would
have simply answered : " Because it contains the
tombs of the blessed apostles Peter and Paul."

Meantime, distant governors ruling or fighting in
far-off lands under Nero's authority were maintaining the glory of the Roman name.   The " British

5

Warrior Queen " was defeated by the Roman general. Distant Armenia received at the hands of the Romans a Parthian prince for their king, who came in person to Rome to receive his crown and promise loyalty. The Frisians, ancestors of the modern Dutch, sent ambassadors to Rome, who eagerly took seats in the Circus among the senators, because they were told that such seats were reserved for friends of the Roman People. But Nero showed little gratitude to governors and generals, and an unwise contempt for the Senate. This want of care and prudence brought about his end. A brave Gaul, Vindex, turned his arms against Nero's forces. Vindex was defeated and slain. But his fellow-conspirator, Galba, was already advancing from Spain. Nero fled, was pursued, and died the death of a coward. His name was held in hatred after his death, yet a few loved his memory and decked his tomb with flowers. Rome survived his evil deeds. Her day of decline from the height of worldly glory had not yet come. And most unwittingly, the Emperor, whom many of his and of after times have thought of as Antichrist, had laid the foundations of the City of Saints and Martyrs.

CHAPTER IV

TRAJAN AND HADRIAN

I F it were our business to take note of all the great men and interesting events that belong to the story of Rome, I should have much to say about the times that followed Nero's death : not about his immediate successors—there were three new emperors in succession in one year, and none of them very remarkable in any way—but about those who laboured, in the city itself and in wars at a distance, to bring about a state of order and of dignity after civil wars and dissensions and general confusion. But as we are only choosing out a few persons and a few notable moments as they pass along on the stream of time, I will but stop for a minute to notice two brothers who ruled over the Empire shortly before the other two emperors of whom I wish to speak more particularly. These two brothers were Titus and Domitian, sons of the Emperor Vespasian—the emperor who came after the three unsuccessful would-be emperors of whom I have just spoken. Vespasian tried in most ways to go back to the ideas and principles of Augustus. Titus and Domitian were often quoted afterwards as showing how different from one another two brothers can be. Titus was kindly, generous—*too* generous, perhaps, some of us would think—a universal favourite. But the chief thing that we have to remember about him is the great war that he put an end to after his father had been carrying it on for some time. From him came the final destruction of the Temple at Jerusalem, and the utter ruin of the Jewish people, of which we read terrible warnings and forebodings in some parts of the New Testament. Within the triumphal arch in Rome set up in honour of Titus, we may still see carved in stone the great candlestick with seven branches, which had been for long a very sacred part of the temple furniture, and which Titus carried away to Rome.

Titus died young, and was succeeded by his brother Domitian, one of the worst-hated men in all history. We hear no good accounts of him from any quarter, though it seems that some among the soldiers had a liking for him, and the chief historians who wrote about him were not always entirely fair in bestowing praise and blame. His worst fault seems to have been his readiness to suspect all around him of having evil designs. He had no children, and he feared lest some of the great men should wish to make away with him and reign in his stead. He felt jealous of those who were

doing more for the Empire than he was. Our own
island had been for the first time really conquered,
and was beginning to enjoy peace and prosperity
under a brave and capable governor, Agricola. The
jealousy felt by Domitian when he heard of Agricola's
great deeds led him to recall a man who might, he
thought, become dangerous. But the greatest mistake he made was to depart from the policy of
Augustus as to the Senate. You remember how
Augustus had always treated the Senate with
marked respect, and had always left it some show
of authority, and in certain matters a little real
authority too. This had generally been the policy
of the wiser among his successors, though perhaps
one could hardly expect that as time went on people
should not come to see that after all the government
had changed, and was no longer a republic but a
monarchy, that its emperors were much more than
first magistrates of one great city. Yet this gives no
excuse to Domitian for insulting the Senators in
every way, calling them in or turning them out as
pleased his fancy, and making them feel that their
very lives depended on his goodwill. The Senators
showed very little spirit or inclination to defend
their rights. Yet when Domitian was murdered by
a conspiracy within his own household, the Senate
rejoiced, and welcomed as emperor a worthy old
man named Nerva.

But the reign of Nerva was short and troubled.
Evil men had gained the upper hand, and well-

meaning as he was, he had to give way and take advice which he felt to be bad. However, he was able to do one good thing. He adopted as his son, and left as his successor, a man who had the power and the will to restore the glory of the Roman arms and to bring back order to the Roman world. This was the Spaniard, Trajan.

But was it not strange that a Spaniard should be placed at the head of the State? It will seem less strange if you remember what we have already seen in the case of Seneca and his father—that natives of provinces that had for some time been under Rome, might, if they had come to hold positions of trust and authority, feel themselves to be Roman citizens, bound to the City by close ties of loyalty, yet not entirely forgetful of the land and people from which they had come. It was these provincials, with Roman training and Roman ideas, that brought fresh life to the State. Trajan himself was a noble specimen of the class. His personal appearance, which we may know well from the numerous statues raised to him, shows a firm will without harshness, the bearing of a soldier with the intelligence of a statesman, and an air of authority which marks him as a real ruler of men. A prince who is quite sure of himself need not dread the appearance or even the reality of liberty in his subjects. Under Trajan, the Senators of Rome felt that they had a governor who would always treat them with courtesy and respect, and listen to all that they had to say. Many a long hour the Emperor sat in the senate-house, listening to weary harangues on his own virtues or on the evil deeds of men to be brought to punishment. He solemnly promised never to put a Senator to death. He received the consulship with the old forms, and seemed to regard it as a great honour to have it conferred on him. He ordered that in voting, senators should express their mind in writing, so as not to be overawed by him. Towards the citizens, generally, he showed an earnest desire for their good. He discouraged the bad habit of inducing rich men to leave money to the Emperor in their wills. He arranged a plan by which money belonging to the State should be lent to farmers for the improvement of their lands, and what they paid for the use of it should go to a fund for maintaining poor children. On many coins of Trajan we see little boys and girls being brought to him for protection and help, and though one of his motives in supporting young citizens may have been to secure, in future days, a larger number of healthy soldiers for the State, yet it is worth while to notice that from about this time, even before the spirit of Christianity had made itself widely felt, a greater regard was paid to the health and welfare of young children, as well as of the poor and the distressed.

But it was not chiefly as a gentle and just ruler that Trajan was to figure in history. The great monument set up to his honour in Rome is a perpetual memorial of the mighty deeds he did in

war. This is a very lofty column, with a series of
military scenes running round it to the top where
the Emperor's statue—now unfortunately lost—used
to stand. We learn more about Roman arms and
dress and ways of living and of fighting from these
carvings than from any amount of description that
we can get from ancient writers. The chief wars
of Trajan were with a brave people, the Dacians,
who inhabited the lands just north of the Danube,
chiefly in the region we now call Hungary. On the
column we see charges of cavalry, building of forts,
distribution of honours to the soldiers, sieges of
cities, cruel Dacian women torturing Roman
prisoners—a fine bridge spanning the river; the
Dacian king, Decebalus, making submission to the
Emperor after the first war; the same heroic king
stabbing himself when all hope was gone, after the
second war. It was a cruel war, as all such wars
must be, but it was not merely a war of destruction
and overthrow. When it was over Trajan planted
colonies of Romans in the conquered territory, who
for a long time kept the boundary line safe, and
gradually taught the barbarous nations beyond to
respect Rome and to desire to share in her civilisation.

In this war Trajan both proved himself to be a
bold and skilful general, and gave his soldiers experience in the hardships and the excitements of war.
The expedition which he undertook some years later,
and which is likewise commemorated on carved

TRAJAN SACRIFICING.

tablets in Rome, was against the old enemy of Rome, the Parthians. The King of Parthia had lately been setting a relative of his own on the throne of Armenia. Trajan subdued the Armenians and then marched eastwards as Alexander had done, while the Great King fled into Media. Trajan marched as far as Babylon, and declared that Armenia, Assyria, and Mesopotamia were all provinces of the Roman Empire. He even seems to have meant to destroy the kingdom of Parthia itself. But he experienced, as other great generals have done, that it is one thing to overrun a country, quite another to conquer it. Rebellions rose behind him. He gave a king to the Parthians—one of their own royal family—and began to return eastward. But he reached no further than the province of Cilicia, where death overtook him.

The Column in Rome is not the only visible witness to Trajan's greatness. Within the City are the ruins of the great Forum, or market-place, he built for the citizens. Aqueducts and bridges, strong forts in distant and lonely places mark his forethought. Many useful buildings in the Roman provinces confirm what we learn from those who knew him as to his ceaseless vigilance with regard to the well-being of those provinces. Indeed, my chief reason for bringing him before you, apart from his interesting character, is that he and his successor Hadrian helped on the process by which men came ever more to regard Rome as the *Middle* of the

World, certainly, but by no means the *whole* of the world.

A monument as interesting as the Column itself is the collection of letters from and to Trajan, relating to the affairs of the province of Bithynia, while the learned and conscientious Pliny was governor there. Bithynia was a very important province on' the south-western shores of the Black Sea. It contained many cities which had been great and powerful once, though now their glory had diminished, and Emperor and governor were alike anxious to restore their prosperity in every way. But what seems strange to us is that in those days, so long before telegraphs and steamboats had lessened all distances, Pliny must needs write to Trajan to ask his advice about all manner of little details. May this town have a fire-brigade ? How is that one to secure a better water supply ? In a third there is a sewer—though people call it a river—running down the main street ; what is to be done with it ? Then among all these inquiries, reasonable or unreasonable, uninteresting except as illustrations of the life of these times and the character of the correspondents, we come upon one of startling interest : what is to be done with the Christians ?

Pliny seems not to have had much to do with any Christians before he went to the East. Some there were, of course, to be found in Rome, though the stories we hear of a persecution under Domitian are not to be relied upon. But they must have been much more numerous in the Asiatic provinces, where were the " Seven Churches in Asia " to whom St. John wrote the Revelation, and many churches that had been founded by St. Paul or his immediate successors. Certainly Pliny found a good many in Bithynia, and he wrote to ask the Emperor how he was to deal with them : whether any difference should be made between strong and weak, old and young, obstinate or ready to recant ; whether people were to be punished simply for *being* Christians, or whether the name in itself were no ground for the condemnation of an otherwise innocent person. He describes the course he has hitherto pursued : when people have been mentioned to him as being Christians, he has asked them whether this were true. If they confessed it, under threats of punishment, two or three times, and persisted in remaining Christians, he has sent them to pay the penalty of their obstinacy, except in the case of Roman citizens, who must be sent to the City for judgment. In course of time accusations had multiplied. A list of names of suspected persons had been sent to him —he knew not from whom. When these persons were questioned, some said that they were not and never had been Christians. These, in the governor's presence, were ordered to call upon the gods, to burn a little incense before the images of the gods and of the Emperor, and to curse the name of Christ. Then they were let go. Others had said hesitatingly that they were, or confessed that they had once been

Christians, but they were willing to adore the gods and the Emperor and to tell the governor wherein their crazy superstition, as he considered it, consisted. They used, they said, to meet before dawn on an appointed day, to sing a hymn to Christ, and to take an oath among themselves to keep from theft and guile and all evil ways. Afterwards they had met again for a common meal. (This was probably not the Lord's Supper, but the Agape, or Feast of Love, observed in the early Church). This practice, however, they had given up since the Emperor had sent orders to put down all combinations and societies. (He had even objected to the fire-brigade which Pliny had suggested. Despots, even the best and kindest, are naturally unfavourable to everything like a secret society.) Pliny had put two slave-girls to the torture, but they had not thrown more light on the subject. He was evidently puzzled, yet persuaded that it was high time to do something, as before he had taken some measures the temples had become almost deserted.

In reply, Trajan commended Pliny for what he had done, but declined to give any definite and strict rules. The Christians were not to be hunted up, and if brought to judgment, were to be allowed an opportunity of abjuring their religion. Above all, Trajan expresses abhorrence of using anonymous letters against anybody. Yet Christianity was to be accounted a crime, and those who persisted in it were to be punished.

It is clear from these letters that both Trajan and Pliny wanted to be fair, that they regarded as dangerous and unlawful any departure from the recognised worship of the national gods (with, as we see, a religious reverence for the Emperor), and that neither of them had the slightest conception, in spite of Pliny's inquiries, of what Christianity really meant. We often see nowadays how difficult it is for excellent people of different kinds to understand one another. It is a wholesome but humiliating thought for us that "the best" of Emperors, as the Senate justly called Trajan, caused men to die for righteousness' sake. Yet it is some consolation to find that in spite of this fact, Christians of a somewhat later day recognised the goodness of the well-meaning persecutor. In the days of ignorance, when men cared little for the glories of pagan times, and had even less reverence for those who, after Christ had come, had ranged themselves against his followers, the righteous Trajan was one of the very few who seemed to escape the condemnation of an evil world. It was said that one of the best of the Popes, moved by a story of Trajan's justice to a poor widow, had earnestly prayed, and had received in answer an assurance that Trajan's justice had been accepted of God, and that at least this pagan had found the way to heaven open to him. But we must now return to earth and to Trajan's successor.

Hadrian was first-cousin-once-removed to Trajan,

and his grand-nephew by marriage. He had been, it was said, adopted by Trajan during the last days of his life, but this was disputed and some declared the adoption to be a story invented by Trajan's wife. Some resistance was made to his claims, but it was speedily put down.

The two emperors were in most ways very unlike one another, yet in some ways they helped to guide the State in the same direction. The family of Hadrian, like that of his predecessor, came from Spain, though Hadrian himself was born in Rome. Trajan, as we have seen, was a great conqueror. Hadrian began by giving up the newly-formed provinces in the East, and returned to the policy of guarding carefully all that belonged to the Empire without trying to increase it. Yet Hadrian no less than Trajan believed in the need of strict discipline for the soldiers, and personally attended to all the details of their arms, baggage, ambulance and other military arrangements. Trajan was a practical man, who cared little for books. Hadrian was so fond of literature, especially of the Greek writers, that from his childhood he went by the name of "the little Greek." Yet he, too, was a practical man, and while he indulged his poetical and literary fancies, never lost an eye for practical possibilities. We hear, by the way, that his literary taste was not perfect—that his favourite authors were not those who had produced the greatest masterpieces of the world. Yet might not the same be said of many of us who do

HADRIAN.

not think ourselves illiterate? Hadrian certainly encouraged learned and thoughtful men to come to him, even some with whose opinions he did not agree. Trajan made much of the Senate and of republican forms. Hadrian did so likewise as far as appearances went. But his government was really more king-like than that of any of his predecessors. Trajan, as we have seen, paid great attention to the government of the provinces, but he seems to have used his influence and authority from a distance, by writing. Hadrian preferred to be ceaselessly travelling about, seeing what was wanted here, there, and everywhere, supplying needs (especially where earthquakes had wrought havoc), contributing liberally to adornment, amusing himself at the same time and indulging his restless curiosity. Both alike loved justice and right, and both alike provided for the succession (unless the story of Trajan's negligence is true) in such fashion that the government of the Empire might be efficiently carried on after their death.

There were only two serious wars in which Hadrian had to take part. Quite early in his reign some of the tribes on the Danube tried to throw off the yoke that Trajan had imposed upon them. They were soon subdued, and in these regions at least Hadrian made more secure what his predecessor had accomplished. Far more important was a war in which he engaged towards the end of his reign, to put down the last rebellion of the Jews. In several provinces they had risen, but their own land was the scene of the fiercest struggle. Of late the hopes of a coming Messiah and a new kingdom had arisen. Hadrian, tolerant enough when he saw no danger to the State, showed himself severer towards this people than had some of their worst persecutors before him. He prohibited their rites, tried to crush out their very existence, and finally took Jerusalem, expelled the Jews, and renamed the sacred city after himself (Ælia Capitolina). This may seem the more strange because towards the Christians Hadrian was actually more liberal than Trajan. He ordered on one occasion that no Christians were to be punished except for crimes. If this rule had been followed everywhere, there would, of course, have been a satisfactory toleration, since no Christian could object if his brothers in the faith suffered for their own faults. But a set of orders issued by an emperor for one time and place were not thereby current generally. It is quite possible that in some places, where the people were strongly prejudiced against the Christians and the rulers sought to please the people, persecutions may have gone on, while in other regions there may have been complete religious liberty. Generally, however, the Church had peace in Hadrian's days, and leisure to form gradually its system of government and of teaching. Hadrian was apparently clever enough to see that Christianity did not threaten the State, but that the Jews could not be made to fit into any orderly system of imperial government as he conceived it.

In his system of government, Hadrian made some changes which bore fruit afterwards and helped to bring about the fall of Augustus' system. Under him, lawyers were favoured, and the laws made in some ways more regular and settled. But the great point to notice is that he liked to give the general business of government—the management of public money, and of settling questions as they arose—to men belonging to the equestrian order, that is, of the rank next below that of the senators. Some of his predecessors had worked chiefly through their freedmen—whom nobody held in much respect. Now a post in the Emperor's service became something that Roman gentlemen liked to obtain for themselves or their sons, and in course of time these government officials and clerks became a body of specially qualified people, entirely dependent on the Emperor, and *really* much more important than the senators who ranked above them. The Senate was there for show, the Emperor's councillors and ministers were for use. It was as if a neat and strong building had been reared within an old and crumbling one, so that if the ancient walls should fall, the inhabitants might still be in shelter and safety.

Hadrian's journeys occupied the greater part of his reign. He first visited Gaul, Germany, Britain, Spain, North Africa, Asia Minor, and Greece. After rather more than a year in Rome he started again for Greece, and went on eastward into Syria, Egypt, and Arabia. It was when in the East that he was obliged to go and quell the revolt in Judæa. In our own island he left his trace in the Great Wall running from the Solway Frith to the mouth of the Tyne, with "mile-houses," or camps, at regular intervals, and farther apart more luxurious abodes, with hot-water apparatus and other arrangements by which natives of the sunny South could be induced to face the cold northern air. It is not likely that in making this fortification Hadrian meant to abandon the country between it and the older line of forts between the Forth and the Clyde. Probably the reduction of what we call the Lowlands of Scotland seemed likely to prove an easier task when the Wall was there, and the wild tribes of the North could hope for no help from those of the South. Wherever Hadrian went, the frontier line was strengthened and public buildings arose. Naturally the place where the "little Greek" felt most at home was Greece itself, the sacred city of Eleusis, which he greatly beautified, and Athens, where he took the title and dress of Archon. He did not here, however, merely try to dream the old days back again. With the curious presumption which marks some clever men who do not think or feel very deeply, he set himself up for a new founder of Athens. To the south-east of the Acropolis he found the foundations and part of

the walls of a temple that had been begun hundreds of years ago, in honour of Olympian Zeus.
This temple Hadrian completed in very magnificent
fashion. A statue of himself was placed within,
along with that of the greatest of the gods. A
festival was founded in honour of the god and of
the Emperor together. At a short distance were
ranged innumerable statues of Hadrian, the over-
turned pedestals of which still commemorate the
cities of Europe and Asia which made their gift to
this semi-divine man. Not content with this, he
set up an arch between the old city and the part
of which he desired to constitute himself the
founder, having on one side the inscription,
"This is the Old City of Theseus," and on the other,
"This is the City of Hadrian, not of Theseus."
" Little Greek," we are tempted to cry, " you are
able to understand much of the art and the learning
and the great achievements of old days. But are
you able really to venerate and to love the wisdom
and the beauty that inspired the patriots and the
thinkers and the statesmen of Athens when she was
at her best ? "

In Italy, too, between Rome and the beautiful little
city of Tibur, Hadrian made a wonderful building
—palace, barracks, and museum in one, and there
he deposited many of the precious things he had
gathered in his travels. There were to be seen
walking and conversing together many philosophers
and men of the world, and among them the able

man whom Hadrian had appointed to succeed him, and the noble boy who was to come next. His restless life came to an end in a villa near the lovely Campanian Sea. As he lay, in great suffering, he composed a little poetical farewell to his soul :

> " Tell me, poor little wandering sprite,
>   Whither art flitting amain ?
> Guest of the Body and friend so bright,
> Now all trembling, chill, and white,
>   Never to laugh again."

Like Augustus, he had played his part well. He had already prepared for himself a magnificent resting-place. On the other side of the Tiber from Rome a magnificent round building had arisen. Here his body, after all its journeyings, was laid to rest, and other members of the imperial family shared the great mausoleum. It had as varied a history as that of the emperor who built it. It became a fortified tower and a prison, and was surmounted by the statue of an angel, from which it still has its name. One would like to be able to amuse its builder with the story of the many strange events which occurred in and around it. But we are still in the old imperial times, and may take our leave of these two great emperors recollecting once more how both of them raised Rome in the eyes of the world by thinking, in their wars and government, not only of Rome, not only of Italy, but of all the multifarious cares and needs of the distant cities and countries that acknowledged Rome as their head and as the Middle of the World.

CHAPTER V

THE SEVERI

I INTENDED to wait for the coming of another notable person in the history of Rome and of the world, and to tell you of the very great change which came about when the Roman Empire became Christian. But as I was preparing to turn away from pagan Rome, with some of the regret which one feels on quitting a grand country into which one has made many delightful excursions, I was struck by the figure of a youth, whom one of the later emperors, seeing his predecessors pass as in a dream before him, perceived sitting apart, weeping and bemoaning his hard fate. This boy had for a long time interested me, and it seemed to me that though he did nothing much to alter the history of the world, yet we might spend a little while profitably in his company and in that of the group of people to whom he belongs, because if we know them, we know about certain ways of thinking and living which we do not come across earlier, and

which help us in some ways to understand what
happened later.   More than that, they set us
dreaming as to what *might* have happened if
some things had gone a little differently, and
though such dreams are idle, they may sometimes, like the dreams we read of in ancient
stories, be capable of a wise interpretation.   But
those of my readers who care only for great acts
and visible changes, had better, after reading what
I have to say of the founder of the family I am to
tell about, a really capable and active man, pass on
to the next chapter.

After Hadrian there came in succession two
emperors of whom the first had adopted the second
as his son, the Antonines, generally called Antoninus
Pius and Marcus Aurelius.   You may see very fine
busts of both of them in the British Museum, in the
left-hand gallery as you enter, a very chamber of
delights for those who want to know not only what
the Emperors did, but what they looked like.   For
at this time, though men had lost the power of
making works of the very noblest kind of art—of
producing dignified statues of the gods and designing great temples—the art of portraiture was flourishing.   Marcus has also left us a word-portrait of his
adoptive father, of the kind that makes one feel
thankful that such men can be found in the world ;
and another word-portrait of his own noble spirit,
its struggles and aspirations, and deep though not
joyous confidence, in the thoughts he wrote down

for his own eye alone. Both the Antonines were busy men, with multitudes of affairs to attend to, and Marcus had to do a good deal of fighting against barbarous German tribes. But after him there came a change. He, unfortunately, did not continue the *adopting* system, and was succeeded by his own son, a man unlike his father in every way, with tastes lower than Nero's for the chariot-races of the amphitheatre, and a horrible inclination to suspect every one around him. After a reign of thirteen years, this bad son of a good father was murdered, and a worthy old Senator set on his throne. But this old man soon gave offence by his determination to keep the Imperial (or Prætorian) Guards in order. He was attacked in his palace by the unruly soldiers, and replaced by a miserable creature of their own. The imperial power had fallen low indeed, but there was at least one man alive capable of restoring it.

This was an African, Septimius Severus, a man who had had experience in fighting, and was now governor of the countries between the Danube and the Adriatic Sea. On hearing of what had been done, he persuaded the army under him to come with him to Rome and avenge the death of good old Pertinax. This was easy enough. The would-be emperor set up by the Guards made no stand at all, and very soon Severus found himself Emperor by decree of the Senate. But he had still some formidable difficulties to overcome. Two other pretenders had started up, one in Britain, the other in the far East. With great wariness, Severus pretended to negotiate with one of these while he attacked the other, and after a short civil war, both were overcome and put to death. Then Severus had scope to carry out his ideas as to the government of Rome and the Empire. He was more of a soldier than any emperor there had been since Trajan, and was exceedingly popular with the army. In some respects he may have been dangerously indulgent to the soldiers, but at least he broke the spirit of the troublesome Prætorian Guards by breaking up their organisation, and admitting men from the provinces to their ranks, and he made the soldiery capable of carrying on campaigns against the distant Parthians, as well as against the rebellious Jews, Egyptians, and Britons. He was not a mere soldier or conqueror, but had reasonable schemes for maintaining a frontier. In the East he made a strong border-province in the land between the Tigris and the Euphrates. In our own country, traces of his northern fortifications are still to be seen. But what we ought specially to notice here is that, so far as he could, he reduced the differences between Italy and the provinces. He paid little heed to the Senate, which always disliked him. He spoke Latin with an African accent, and such a circumstance was not in his favour with pure-blooded Romans, though in the case of emperors who had been outwardly respectful to the Senate and the other institutions of Old Rome such minor points were forgotten. We have seen how he admitted non-Italians into the Prætorian Guard. He gave a new character to the Prætorian Præfect, who had been a military captain and now became a kind of Prime Minister and Lord Chancellor. He paid no heed to the fancies of the Romans where they did not seem reasonable. He would not allow that in and near the City his authority was different in character from that which he exercised in the provinces. He gave the rights of Italians to many communities beyond the sea. In short, he followed what we should call a policy of *cosmopolitanism*, in which distinctions between all countries and communities should gradually be done away. Such a line of action, you would say, must make Rome herself cease to be the Middle of the World. But Rome was important in so many ways that as soon as she lost some of her old honours, other distinctions came to be conferred upon her, as we shall see by and by.

I might have said that this story is to be in great part concerned with three great ladies. Now you may have noticed that in the history of the Greeks and Romans, in their best times, there is not very much said about ladies. There are a few prominent women, like Atossa the wife of Darius, and Cleopatra Queen of Egypt, but they generally belong to distant lands. You may remember how we saw that in Athens, ladies who were respected spent almost all their time indoors.

In Sparta they had more liberty, and their bodies
were well developed, but their minds were not
much cultivated, any more than those of Spartan
men in early times. In Rome, the mother of the
house was very much respected, yet she was entirely
under the power of her father before she married,
and afterwards entirely under that of her husband
or of the head of her family, whoever he might be.
Women's life was even more unlike that of men
than it is in our days. Women had no particular
place in society so long as all the interests of men
were military or political. As time went on, however, many states lost their independence and thus
their citizens became less absorbed in politics ; and
at the same time, long stretches of peace gave
opportunity for quiet home life as well as for
social display. This social display was greatly
encouraged by the beginnings of court life, in
the kingdoms of Alexander's successors in the
East, and later in the Roman Empire. And now
we begin to see women becoming more independent,
better educated, and in many ways of greater power
in society. The old laws were gradually relaxed so
that a Roman lady might own property and be her
own mistress. The Romans generally, as you know,
were opposed to change, and in this case there may
have been some reason for their opposition, as the
Roman ladies in becoming emancipated did not
always realise that greater power must mean
greater responsibility. Augustus had strict notions

as to the duty of women to stay at home and spin and weave ; but we have seen that his ideas were not successfully carried out in the case of his own daughter. As, however, the Roman Empire became extended to take in so much of the world, especially of the civilised East, the old Roman strictness tended, for better and for worse, to vanish away. The ladies I am to tell you about were Syrians, yet they helped for a time to determine and regulate the fortunes of the Roman world.

There was another change gradually taking place which *seemed* likely to end by making Rome cease to be the Middle of the World—though how things were prevented from coming to that pass we shall see as we go on. The change I mean was in men's ways—and women's ways too—of regarding religion. In old times the religions of the various states had been sufficient for everybody. People who used their minds began, in course of time, to disbelieve the old stories of the gods, but it was thought advisable, even by the best men, to keep to the old cere-monies. Yet as knowledge and leisure and all that we call civilisation increased, the desire grew ever stronger for some belief as to the relation of man and of the world to the power or powers that rule over both—a belief that might determine the principles of right action towards that Power and towards one's fellow-men ; and satisfy those feelings of exultation, of awe, and of humiliation which naturally express themselves in the sacred poetry

of the Hebrew Psalmists, but which found little
scope in the cut-and-dried ceremonies of ordinary
national and civic worships, among either Greeks
or Romans.   The result of all this was that
educated people began to look for their religion
to the philosophic sects, and, as you know, the
Stoics at least had something to give them.
Meantime, those who had less knowledge and
grosser tastes began to adopt the various foreign
worships which, as we have seen, had begun to
find votaries in Rome, and which were certainly
more exciting and had more to say about marvels
on earth and greater marvels in a life after death
than any of the recognised religions.   But both
the philosophers and the followers of Oriental
worships kept to the religion of Rome, and
worshipped the Emperor or his Genius.   It was
in this respect—that they could not be so accom-
modating—that the Christians, as we have seen,
stood alone and incurred danger.   But we must
so far try to enter into the minds of the people
of the Roman Empire as to understand that
Christianity was not the *only* religion that penetrated deeper than the older systems had done,
and led men to think more of their relation to
God and of their prospects in a future life.   Not
that these foreign religions, or even the various
philosophies, worked entirely for good.   True, they
helped to break down barriers between nations, to
make men think of their fellow-men as brothers,

to be more humane and merciful. You see this especially in the greater efforts made to relieve the poor and to care for children, such as were carried out by the Emperor Trajan. In some cases, they helped men to rise to the thought of One God, the ruler and judge and father of all. But there could be no greater mistake than to suppose that religion is always a good thing in itself. To many people becoming religious meant the indulgence of a passion for excitement which worked for evil rather than for good in their ordinary life. But it is worth noticing that the general interest felt in religion was a great help in the spread of Christianity. It was a danger too, as in very early times we come across curious sects that made a strange mixture of Christian and pagan and dreamy-philosophical ideas in their religious systems. Some who called themselves the Gnostics, or knowing ones, taught very strange doctrines that might have spread far but for the strong position taken up against them by Christians of a plainer sort.

I may here say, that from the death of Trajan till the end of the second century Christians generally had a quiet time, though there may have been per-secutions in various places. Hadrian, as we have seen, once ordered that Christians should not be punished simply as Christians, and though it might be easy under a corrupt governor to find some charge which could be brought against a Christian without simply charging him as such, yet in general the Christians had a right to toleration, and for the most part they were able to exercise it. They used their rest to make progress in various ways. Those in one part were able to have intercourse with those in another, though there were as yet no general councils of the whole Christian body, such as we shall hear of later on. Every large town, and even many a small town, had its bishop, assisted by presbyters or priests and various inferior clergy, for the distinction between clergy and laity had by that time become pretty clear and definite. Their ritual was as yet very simple. They had their own burying grounds in the city of Rome and elsewhere, and kept carefully the bodies of those who, they believed, were shortly to rise again. Especially they tended the tombs of those who had suffered for their faith, and held gatherings near them as in a sacred place. These under-ground burying-places thus grew often into places of worship, especially in times of persecution or popular disfavour, and from them have been brought carvings and paintings, not first-rate in character—the early Christians were not great artists—but interesting to us as showing us some of their religious ideas, and especially how they gave new and Christian meanings to old signs and even to some stories of pagan mythology. Meantime many men had become Christians who were better educated than those of earlier genera-tions, and they made it their business to explain their faith to the ruling powers and to educated people generally. Only a few years ago, the work of one of these Apologists, as they are called, which learned men had heard of but never seen, came to light. It was addressed to the great emperor who succeeded Hadrian, and if he read it he probably tossed it aside, thinking, " It is odd for these ·Christians to be making themselves out to be philosophers ; yet perhaps they are not more unreasonable than other people." For apologists of this kind could not make the most of the really strong points of their religion. But we must go back to the Roman Emperors and the pagan life of old Rome.

What Severus was doing in government and politics, his wife—the first of the clever ladies of whom I have to speak—was doing in society. She was a Syrian lady, with no particular attachment to Rome, but with conspicuous social qualities such as helped her to form a brilliant, cosmopolitan society in and around the imperial court. Severus had been induced, it was said, to make Julia Domna his wife by the advice of astrologers—for it was part of the change in men's minds of which I have been speaking that more credit was now attached than a century before to dreams and omens and to those who studied such things. But probably Julia's beauty and great intelligence did more than her horoscope in making her the bride of an emperor. Julia was a mistress of the art of conversation ; she had opinions on all subjects from religious reforms down to the smallest details of life. She loved to gather round her people of all nations, and to receive compliments from them. "Julia the Philosopher" was a name by which she liked to be called. Her influence in practical matters was probably greater after the death of her husband, with whose advisers she could not always agree. Severus and Julia had two sons, Caracalla and Geta, who from early life (by whose fault we cannot say) had always felt and indulged a bitter hatred against one another. When Severus died at York (after chastising the fierce Caledonians of the Scottish Highlands) it was proposed that the brothers should share the Empire between them. No plan of division, however, was likely to be successful. Very soon Geta, the mother's favourite, was murdered by his brother or his brother's attendants in the presence of Julia herself. But though she loved her murdered boy, she loved power more—at least so we should judge from her readiness to be reconciled to the murderer, and the honour she enjoyed throughout his reign.

Caracalla was a soldier like his father, and so far as he had any policy it was like his father's, but he seems to have allowed a large share in the direction of things to his mother, while he traversed the provinces at the head of his armies. Julia was not satisfied with being merely the Emperor's mother, and so shining with a reflected

light. We find the titles ascribed to her, " Mother
of the Senate," " Mother of the Country," " Mother
of the Camps." It may be partly by her influence
that an edict was passed which, if the way to
it had not been gradually prepared long beforehand, might seem indeed to change the position of
Rome towards the rest of the Empire ; all the rights
and duties of Roman citizenship were conferred on
the freeborn subjects of the provincial governments.
This seems a very liberal measure—and so it was—
but to the Emperor it opened possibilities of getting
more money and more military service from some
of the distant provinces. Meantime Rome was
beautified by magnificent buildings, and the government saw no need for economy.

In the year 217 A.D., Caracalla, who, though
popular with the soldiers, had made many enemies
by his cruelty and injustice, was murdered while
travelling in the furthermost eastern provinces. His
mother, rather than retire into a private station, put
an end to her life in a way that must require an iron
will—by voluntary starvation. But she had relatives
who soon succeeded in thrusting from power the
usurper Macrinus, who was not a favourite with the
soldiers. A sister of Julia Domna, Julia Maesa,
like herself in ambition and in activity, had, on
the death of Caracalla, been exiled to their original
home, Emesa in Syria. Here was a temple of a
sun-god, El-Gabal, whom we may regard as similar
in character to the Baal against whose detestable

7

rites the Israelites were so often warned before the days of their captivity. Maesa had two daughters, each of whom had been married to a Syrian and had now one son. It is a curious thing that the original names of these two boys are differently reported, by different historians, since afterwards one of them was always called by the name of his god, and the other by that of his favourite hero. We will keep to these names, and call them Elagabalus and Alexander. The elder sister, Soæmias, mother of Elagabalus, was a frivolous and foolish woman who cared for nothing but pleasure. Her boy, a handsome youth of fourteen, acted as priest in the temple of the Sun-god. The younger sister, Mammæa, was a woman of thoughtful, earnest, and cultivated mind, who showed through all her life a deep devotion to the best interests of her son, Alexander, and an intelligent sympathy with all that was best in the world in which she had to live. The old grandmother, determined that the boy Elagabalus should be made Emperor, caused people to believe that he was the son, not of his reputed father, but of the murdered Caracalla. She presented him to the troops who were quartered near, and they received him with enthusiasm. Soon afterwards the whole family were in Rome, and Elagabalus was Emperor. He ruled for about three years, but all that time he thought of himself first as priest, and only in the second place as Emperor. This does not mean that

he was the same kind of king as our Edward the
Confessor, and others who have cared more for
pious meditation and devotion than for active duty,
In the religion of the Syrians and the worship of
the god symbolised by the great black stone which
Elagabalus brought to Rome, there was much to
stir up excitement and to make the worshippers
forget their ordinary life in deeds of wild folly, but
nothing that taught any duties towards one's self or
one's neighbours. The story of these three bad
years shows us the Roman Senate and nobles at the
lowest point of degradation, for it seemed almost
more despicable for a man who bore a good old
name to don a Syrian dress and take part in Syrian
rites than it had seemed for such a man to share
and applaud the sports of Nero. They help us to
understand, too, something of the horror in which
the Hebrew prophets held the worship of Baal, and
the character of Syrian queen-mothers like Jezebel
and Athaliah. Soæmias was like these princesses
in the rites practised by herself and her son. But
she seems to have been too lazy and self-indulgent
to interfere much in the government, though she
and her mother actually intruded sometimes into
the Senate. Old Julia Maesa would have restrained
the extravagance of her grandson if she could have
done so, but he had gone too far to be recalled ; in
fact we may say that he had fairly lost his senses.
One good thing she brought to pass. Elagabalus
was persuaded to adopt, and thus to nominate as

his successor, his cousin Alexander, only a few years younger than himself. Before long the young Emperor was assassinated by some of those whose hatred he had incurred by his odious conduct. His murderers were encouraged, it is *said*, by Maesa and Mammæa. Of course we should like to disbelieve the accusation so far as Mammæa is concerned, and it cannot be regarded as proved. Yet even she may have been driven to desperation by the fear that her own promising boy might be led astray and perhaps destroyed by those who held the supreme power, and who could not be punished for their wickedness in any lawful way.

In any case the bad dream was over, and the imperial throne was now held by a boy who had been carefully trained in good letters and good morals, and who had a real sense of the duties of his position. Alexander, in spite of his mixed race, felt himself to be a Roman ruler. He hated the flattery and cringing manners which had been of late the fashion among the courtiers. He had been well instructed in the best writers of Greece and Rome, and was a good musician. He had no sympathy with the Syrian modes of worship, but restored the Roman national gods to their previous place of honour. Yet, being a man of strong religious feeling, he wanted some support and inspiration such as the old religions could not afford. He probably obtained his ideas as to religion from his mother, Mammæa. She was one of those people,

of whom a good many were to be found at that
time, who believed that most religions contained
some truth and that none contained the whole, and
that by choosing different portions from different
systems one might secure the good of all without
the evil of any. In the course of your historical
studies, you will find people living at many different
times who have made a similar attempt. But we
cannot go into the subject now. It is, however,
interesting as showing some of the first advances
made by the imperial court towards the Christians.

I have spoken of the rest generally enjoyed by
the Christians between the time of Hadrian and
that of Severus. This Emperor, however, strictly
prohibited conversions either to Christianity or
to Judaism, and we read of many martyrdoms,
especially at Alexandria and Carthage, during his
reign. Elagabalus kindly invited the Christians
to worship his sun-god, but seems not to have
troubled himself much about them. Alexander
and Mammæa regarded them with a friendly
eye. Alexander allowed any one who desired it
to join their body, and when an appeal was made
to him concerning a piece of land which certain
victuallers had claimed after Christians had occupied
it for a church, he declared that " it was better that
God should be worshipped there in any fashion
whatsoever than that it should be made over to
people of low character." Some of Alexander's ideas
might seem to many people to have been borrowed

from the Christians, as : Never do to others what
you would not have others do to you (though here
the *not* makes a great difference between this and
the Christian Golden Rule). But Alexander had
no intention of devoting himself to Christianity
exclusively. He regarded Christ as a saint to be
classed among some of the noblest men of an-
tiquity. He had, after his experience of his
cousin's wild orgies, become convinced that human
goodness is more worthy of worship than natural
fruitfulness and beauty. Accordingly, in the chapel
into which he daily went to pray, he set up statues
of great and good men, some in a higher, others
in a lower rank, just as people afterwards came to
distinguish red-letter and black-letter saints. One
of his chief heroes was Alexander the Great, little
as he might seem to resemble him. He recognised
the worth of those gentler virtues which paganism
had generally neglected, and esteemed charity towards the poor of higher worth than liberality
towards temples.

Meantime there were some Christians who were
aware of much that was good in the life and
thoughts of virtuous pagans, just as these liberal
pagans were ready to see some good in Christianity.
I am not thinking now of the strange Gnostic sects
I have mentioned, who invented elaborate systems
that were a confused mixture of pagan and Christian ideas, and had in them very little philosophy
or religion either, and certainly no common sense.

Far more reasonable, charitable, and fruitful were the thoughts of a school of Christian thinkers who dwelt in those days in Alexandria. One of the most thoughtful and amiable among them was the saint and philosopher Origen, who once came on a visit to Mammæa and talked to her about Christian beliefs. These two noble souls, both so ready to discern and reverence that which is good, wherever it might appear, had really much in common. And one of the great "might have beens" of history is the acceptance of a kind of Christianity like Origen's by religious-minded pagan rulers like Alexander and Mammæa. This, however, was not to be.

Meanwhile, in other fields than that of religion, Alexander and his mother were busy with reforms. The Senate had, we have seen, been insulted, degraded, and weakened. Alexander did what could be done to restore its dignity, consulted it habitually, and chose out sixteen of its most experienced members to form a perpetual council. The laws had been set at nought. Alexander gave much of his confidence to men who had made the Law their special study. The whole State was burdened by the heavy expenditure of the last two reigns. Alexander remitted taxes and tried to help the distressed in every way, and to exercise a strict economy. He was naturally generous, but his mother's frugality (for which she had a good excuse) brought on their government the charge of stinginess.   The soldiers had become unruly through over-indulgence. Alexander tried to reduce them to obedience, and once showed great spirit in putting down a mutiny.   Meantime he lived a simple, genial life, devoting part of every day to good reading and to physical exercise, attending strictly to public business, and enjoying the society of clever and worthy people.   He disliked large dinner-parties.   It was "like eating in a theatre or in a circus," he said.   The only fault to be found with him was that of being too deferential to his excellent mother.   She seems to have been jealous of his affection for the Roman wife she had found for him, and the young Empress had to be sent away.   But possibly there were faults on both sides.

Meantime storms were lowering over the frontier lands.   In the East a new power had arisen.   A new dynasty had been founded by the Persian Artaxerxes, who tried to revive the old power of Cyrus.   He had reduced the Parthians under his power and founded an empire which was to be the great rival of Rome for centuries.   Alexander had to lead an army eastward, but he did not justify his name, and though one historian tells us of a great victory he achieved, the campaign can hardly have been a great success.   After his return to Rome he had to start for the Rhine, where the German tribes were moving.   Near the city of Mainz the end came.   There was discontent in the army: some say because Alexander wished to restore discipline, others because Mammæa had interfered and urged a retreat. In any case, a mutiny broke out, and mother and son perished together. Though many fair hopes fell with them, yet we feel that even if they could have prolonged their days and their influence, they could not have accomplished what the times required. Alexander was not a great soldier, and in religion he wanted to mix things that could never go together. Still, whether capable or not, he is one of the most attractive and lovable characters in later Roman History.

CHAPTER VI

CONSTANTINE THE GREAT—CHANGES IN GOVERN-MENT AND IN RELIGION

THE time that 1 wish to speak of next is important rather as a period of great changes than as a time of great men. I do not mean that we have no great men in those days. But the circumstances of the time would have brought about much that was new and unexpected if there had been only little men to carry out the needful changes. Though of course we cannot say that in such a case the changes would have been exactly of the kind that they actually were.

Let us look at the dangers and difficulties which beset the Roman Empire at the time we had reached at the end of our last reading. There seemed a danger of a general break-up. The Empire was so vast that it was most difficult for one man to attend to the needs of all its various parts, unless he had strong and experienced officials under him, and then he needed to be always travelling about to gain information himself and to remind the nations that a Roman Emperor existed. To the east of the lands under Roman sway a new power had arisen, the revived monarchy of Persia, and had become a competitor with Rome for the dominion of the lands between the Tigris and the Euphrates. To the north the German tribes were becoming restless and formidable. Meantime the army was falling beyond the control of the government, and few troops could be relied on to do their duty with strict military obedience. Then there were internal troubles more serious than those which threatened from without. The Roman Senate had ceased to take even that share in public business which had been left to it by Augustus. Not only had Roman society lost its old simplicity —that had happened long before—but it had lost its self-respect and its own marked character. In former times, when Rome had admitted neighbouring communities into her citizen body, the members of these communities had become Romans. Now that the citizenship had been extended universally, there was no distinction, no glory and pride in possessing it. Religion, too, which had been a bond of union, was losing its connection with the Empire. Many people worshipped the genius of the Emperor and the City of Rome and offered sacrifices on behalf of the ruling powers, but there was no strong feeling on the part of religious people towards either the old

national or the new imperial worships. Some, as
we have seen, preferred foreign gods and their cults,
especially Eastern sun-gods. I may add here that
the gods of Egypt were very popular—Isis, Osiris,
Serapis—because Egypt was reverenced as the
home of ancient wisdom. The Christians, constantly increasing in number, were not likely to
rebel while let alone. But while their religion
taught them submission, it was not consistent with
an ardent loyalty towards a heathen Emperor, still
less with patriotic devotion to civic duty. If we
could imagine an enlightened statesman looking
from a distance over all the Roman world, and if
we could suppose ourselves asking him what the
world wanted, we can imagine him answering:
"The army must be made obedient; if Italians or
other citizen soldiers have lost the power or the will
to fight, we must enlist more barbarians. There
must be a division of labour and of authority
among the ruling powers. We want more than one
Emperor and more than one Imperial City, so that
there may be real centres of government near the
frontier, both towards the Persians and towards
the free Germans. And it is time to do away with
the nonsensical notion that the Emperor and the
Senate share the supreme power. Let the Emperor
continue to establish what Hadrian began—a
system of civil servants, of high officials, divided
into grades and subject to himself alone. Let him
show himself to be, what he really is, a magnificent

potentate, not the mere head of a republic. A crown and a ceremonious court will not come amiss. And why should he not surround himself with a religious halo too? If all the world is becoming Christian, let the Emperor frankly adopt Christianity and make it a State religion. He will then be naturally called upon to decide disputes as to rites and doctrines, and if he plays his cards well, all the bishops will look to him, and unless they are *very* independent in mind, will soon begin to adulate him and use all their influence to strengthen his authority. Let him get the laws gradually revised, too, so that there may be one code for the whole Empire. If these things are done, the Empire may cease to deserve the name *Roman*—yet how far does it merit the name now? —but it will more distinctly become universal, and will take a new lease of life."

It would be too much to expect that any one man should have the judgment and the strength to adopt and to act upon *all* the counsels of our supposed statesman. They were, however, adopted one by one, and in a sense they revived the Empire, though they did not, even in the long run, reduce Rome to an insignificant Italian city.

After the fall of young Alexander Severus there was a time of great confusion. About 250 A.D. a real soldier-emperor, Decius, made a bold resistance to the invading Goths, but fell in battle against them. Not long after, another emperor, Valerian, was

taken prisoner by the King of Persia, and kept by him
in chains. Happily for the Roman world, there came,
after a period of still worse confusion, a succession
of able and warlike rulers, who kept the invaders at
bay and tried to restore law and order. Then there
came a very remarkable emperor, who brought
about some of the changes in administration just
suggested. This was Diocletian, a man whose
parents had been slaves, yet who was the first to lay
aside completely the citizen-mask of Augustus, and
appear as a thoroughgoing autocrat. He wore a
diadem—as only one of his predecessors seems to
have done. He accepted grand-sounding titles,
especially that of *dominus*, or *master*, from which
besides the Spanish *don*, the Italian *donna* and
madonna, so many words in our language are derived with the meaning of *domination*. He wore
purple and jewels even in his slippers, and ordered
that all who approached him should bow to the
ground and should observe the most stringent rules
of politeness. He cannot, however, have done all
this merely from a vulgar desire to seem great, or he
would scarcely have consented to share his powers
with a colleague. But since he had at least sufficient
modesty and prudence to see that he was, with all
his ability, unable to defend and maintain the whole
Empire at the present juncture, he chose a brave but
uneducated man, Maximian, to act as his colleague
with the title of *Augustus*. Under these two were to
be two sub-emperors, as we may call them, with the

title of *Cæsar*. Among the four the different provinces were divided for government and defence, though the powers exercised by the Cæsars in their provinces were not so great as those of the Augusti. On the retirement or death of an *Augustus*, the *Cæsar* subordinate to him was to succeed. Thus the mischief of dynastic rule—the government of unworthy sons succeeding to their nobler fathers—might be avoided. As Diocletian and Maximian were neither of them natives or great admirers of Rome, the Senate of which was no longer even a humble council of the Emperor, they fixed their residences in places whence the frontiers on either side could more easily be reached—Maximian in Milan, Diocletian in Nicomedia, a city of Asia Minor. In one respect, however, Diocletian followed an opposite course from that proposed by our imaginary counsellor. In his reign occurred the last and severest of the persecutions of the Christians, who had of late been spreading their doctrines widely, even within the Emperor's own family. What induced Diocletian, who was generally in favour of mild measures, to act in this one respect with such great harshness is a much-vexed question to this day. Many writers are inclined to lay the chief blame on the Cæsar Galerius. While the four colleagues worked together, matters went fairly well. The western provinces were more than once in extreme danger owing to the movement southward of great confederations of German tribes. Among them were the Alamanni and the Franci, names which sound familiar enough to us, though they have not always denoted the same peoples. Maximian and the Cæsar Constantius had much fighting to do in the countries bordering on the Rhine, and were generally successful. The plan came to be more and more frequently adopted of allowing some barbarian tribes that were willing to submit to Roman governors to settle within the frontier and to withstand their ruder brethren outside. This plan and that of enlisting barbarians in the Roman armies, worked both for good and for evil on the fortunes of the Empire. It helped to ward off dangers for the present. At the same time it enabled the barbarians to learn the use of Roman arms and Roman discipline, and this made the great invasions easier, as we shall see in due time. Meanwhile, Galerius, after suffering a defeat, was victorious in the East, and a satisfactory treaty was made between Rome and Persia.

At length, however, in 305, Diocletian, perhaps wearied of pomp and display and longing for a quiet, natural life, or probably exhausted by the attacks of a disease which must soon incapacitate him for any arduous work, gave up the imperial power and took to growing cabbages on a quiet country estate. He persuaded his colleague, the Augustus Maximian, to abdicate likewise, and two new Cæsars were appointed to fill the vacant places. Such a plan looked well on paper, but facts and the passions of human nature were against it.

Fiery old Maximian had no wish to abdicate, and as soon as he had an opportunity tried to recover his former authority and honours. Then he had a son Maxentius, remarkable for ambition and determination. The Cæsar Constantius Chlorus had likewise a son, Constantine, who had distinguished himself in some of the wars of Diocletian. These men were not likely to be easily set aside in favour of others who were comparatively unknown. A crisis came when Constantius—who, as we have seen, governed well and fought hard in the West—died in Britain, and Constantine, who had with some difficulty joined his father, was acknowledged by the soldiers as his successor. I need not go into the details of the civil war which followed. They are complicated and difficult to grasp. Old Maximian seems to have come from his retirement to support his son, then to have deserted or pretended to desert him; to have made an alliance with Constantine and then to have plotted against him, and provoked a war which ended with his own death at Marseilles. Maxentius ruled from Rome, and made himself hated there till Constantine marched into Italy and defeated him. At one time, no fewer than six men claimed imperial authority. One after another was slain or otherwise removed, till in 313 only two remained, Constantine in the West and Licinius in the East; and in 323, after the final war between the rivals and the death of Licinius, Constantine stood alone at the head of the Roman World,

How, then, can we treat the schemes of Diocletian as preparing the way for the necessary changes that were to come, if his plans failed so utterly? But observe—his plans as to *the succession* failed, as did also his policy of religious persecution, since some of the rivals courted the Christians to help them in the contest. But his ideas of divided administration and of making all the officers of state nominees of the Emperor, and forming what we call a bureaucratic government, were worked out by Constantine when he had the power and the leisure to do so.

The name of Constantine is such a famous one in history, and such momentous events are connected with it, that we cannot help wishing to know more than is actually possible about the man himself— his personal character and the motives from which he acted. In some ways, if we look at his actions and those of his contemporaries, he is well able to stand the comparison. He was a brave and able soldier, as was shown not only in his early campaigns and in the civil wars, but in his determined and generally successful resistance to the Goths and other German hosts. He showed on most occasions an inclination to spare his vanquished foes. As elder brother to a large family of step-brothers and sisters, he seems to have behaved well. His laws show a care for good morals and for the well-being of poor people and young children. But when we find that some of the contemporary church-historians, with exaggerated feelings of natural gratitude, represent him as a hero and a saint, we feel that they are going too far. In fact the best years of Constantine seem to have been those of the earlier and less prosperous part of his career. As he grew old, he seems to have become suspicious and unscrupulous. The greatest blot on his name is the removal by death of his brave young son Crispus, who had done much to help him win the throne, and who seems to have in some way incurred his jealousy. Neither in his ordinary life nor in his religious policy does he seem, on nearer view, worthy of the pedestal on which his ecclesiastical biographers have placed him.

But let us turn to consider the changes which he brought about, the results of which are much more clearly seen than his objects in making them. These are of three kinds : (1) changes in the administration of the government; (2) changes in the centre of government—ultimately involving a change in the capital of the Empire : and (3) changes in religion.

1. With regard to the first set of changes, those in the general administration, it is not easy for us who get most of our information about them from documents drawn up much later, to decide how much of them was due to Constantine, how much to his predecessor Diocletian. We know, however, (i.) that after this time there are at least three grades of officials, with their titles—roughly translated as *illustrious, worshipful,* and *honourable*—scrupulously observed. And we find, as might be expected in an almost Oriental government, that the *court* as distin-

guished from *state* offices are becoming important.
What would Augustus have thought of such an
officer as the "Superintendent of the Sacred Bed-
chamber"?   Perhaps this title was not used till a
generation or two later, but the Court was becoming
more and more the centre to which men looked for
promotion and profit.

(ii.) The whole Empire was divided into four
Præfectures, then again into Dioceses (each under a
Vicar), and these yet again into Provinces, of which
there were in all 116, under men who bore various
titles, sometimes that of Rector.   It is curious to
notice that some terms now used only in an
ecclesiastical sense, once belonged to civil divisions
or governors.   The reason is of course to be found
in the fact that often the organisation of the Church
followed that of the State, and that in the great
breaking-up the civil offices and dignitaries were
lost while the ecclesiastical remained.

(iii.) All the civil and military offices were separated.   A great general was no longer to be a far-
ruling governor, nor should a præfect or his sub-
ordinates have military anthority.   Doubtless the
object of this change was to take away from popular
governors or victorious generals the temptation
to usurp supreme authority.   Unfortunately the
troubles of succeeding times rendered this attempt
ineffectual.

Now all these great officials had to keep up large
establishments, and that of course involved heavy

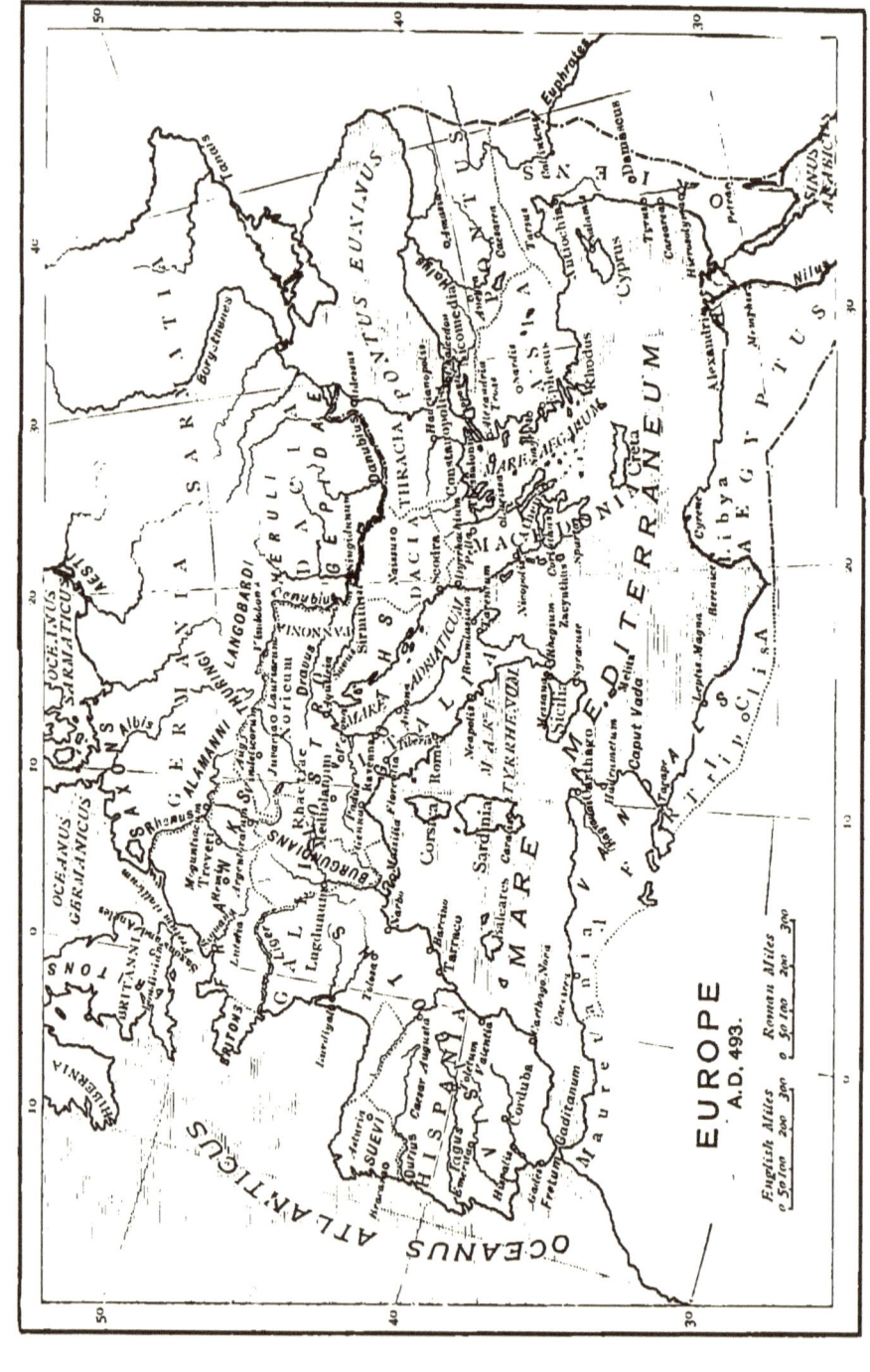

EUROPE
A.D. 493.

English Miles
0 50 100 200 300

Roman Miles
0 50 100 200 300

taxation. A great part of the taxation of the Empire was levied on a select number of citizens of the great towns, who were held responsible for the amount, and had to collect it if they could from their fellow-citizens. No wonder that this method tended to make men anxious to avoid responsible posts, and to crush what remained of local patriotism. One of the ugliest features in the political and social life of the later Empire is the anxiety of people who could pay to obtain immunity from the heavy dues, and the want of that old sense of duty to one's own city which had been the root of all that was noblest in the political life of ancient times.

2. But the change which has left to the world a tangible and a perpetual memory of Constantine is the great city which he founded, or refounded, on the Bosphorus, to be a "new Rome" and to bear his name for ever. Some writers who disliked him represented this step as taken mainly in order to dishonour the ancient city of Rome and to enable Constantine himself to live in imperial dignity and pomp elsewhere. This notion, however, is foolish and based on nothing. In the first place Constantine had no ill-will towards Rome. He enriched the city with baths, and with a triumphal arch, to adorn which—to such a depth had the art of sculpture fallen—he was obliged to steal some reliefs, most likely from Trajan's Forum. And he did not, as is commonly said, raise his new city at once to the rank of her mother, though he

established a Senate there, appointed a special præfect, and beautified it with a circus, a forum, baths,
and all manner of splendid monuments, many of
them, alas! taken from their proper places where
skilful hands had raised them centuries before. In
fact, Constantine was again following on the lines of
Diocletian, and establishing the chief seat of the
ruler of the eastern part of the Empire where he
could with comparative ease reach the eastern frontier. Byzantium had been a great city when it was
an independent Greek colony. Its position made it
the key of the Black Sea and of Asia Minor. Many
wars had turned on the possession of it, and we all
know how at this day it is the great bone of conten-
tion among European powers. By strengthening
and beautifying it, Constantine raised a bulwark to
protect Western civilisation. If he could not see in
what way this bulwark would be effective, we need
not therefore deprive him of the credit of being far-
sighted even as Alexander, whose name-sake city still
witnesses to his greatness.

But did not such a step as this tend to deprive
Rome of her position as Middle of the World?
Strange to say, the result was exactly the opposite of
what might have been expected. A story which was
believed all through the Middle Ages, and by Roman
Catholics still later, though nobody believes it now,
serves at least to illustrate the effect on Rome of
Constantine's new capital. It was said that the
Emperor had suffered grievously from leprosy, and

that no doctor could cure him. But when he appealed to the holy man Sylvester, then Bishop of Rome, the prayers and the miraculous powers of the saint availed to cure the Emperor, who vowed in his gratitude a glorious gift to the Bishops of Rome. The imperial court should be removed to Constantinople in order that the Bishops might reign supreme in old Rome, and the same Bishop was likewise to have power over all islands (the assertion of this claim comes up again and again in history). Now although the story is an impudent invention—for the historians would surely have told us if Constantine had ever had the leprosy, still more if he had made such an extraordinary gift to an ecclesiastical authority—yet there is in it this amount of truth : the ultimate desertion of Rome by the Emperors, which in course of time followed the settlement of Constantine in his new city, left the Bishop, or Pope, as he is called later, the most important person in the City, and her natural champion against barbarian foes. Also the distance between the new centre of imperial and the old centre of ecclesiastical authority enabled the Western Church to maintain an independence with regard to the civil power such as was impossible for the Eastern. Some of the Patriarchs of Constantinople were as courageous in opposition to the Emperors as were the Popes of Rome. But living overshadowed by the palace, they found it harder to maintain their ground.

3. But these considerations bring us to speak of Constantine's third great change :—the adoption of Christianity as the religion of the Empire.

We have already spoken of the bitter persecution which the Christians suffered under Diocletian, and its general cessation during the conflict among the rivals for the Empire. Now both Constantine and his father, Constantius, were well inclined to the Christians. It is possible that Helen, the wife of Constantius, may have been a Christian before her son. According to a curious legend, she visited Palestine, and there received in a dream a revelation of the spot where the cross of Christ was buried under a temple dedicated to Venus. The cross was dug out and a church built over it. But apart from the influence of Helen, of whom we know but little (though that little is good), we have reason to think that Constantius and Constantine both saw that the old religions were dying out, and both thought that it would be a bad thing for the people and the State if no public and authorised religion were followed and no prayers or sacrifices offered on behalf of the ruling powers. Within the time between Constantine's elevation to the Empire and his attainment of sole authority, he issued two edicts allowing complete religious toleration. Not only might the Christians receive new converts but they might hold property in common, and the churches that had been destroyed were to be restored. But Constantine was soon ready to go much further than this. A story was current, resting on his authority only, and therefore likely to be taken or rejected by us according to our opinion of his character for truthfulness. In the anxious time before his great conflict with Maxentius, he saw in the sky the figure of the Cross, with the inscription affixed " By this conquer." During the night Christ appeared to him, and explained to him the meaning of the sign : he was to take the Christian symbol for his military standard. This was the legendary origin of the Labarum or standard-cross which we see on many of the coins of Constantine and his successors. Really, it was a very ancient symbol, to be found in Egypt and elsewhere, but henceforth it always has a Christian meaning, and in its usual form or, indeed, in its second form, it gives a mono-

gram of the first two Greek letters in the name of Christ. However this may be, Constantine, when he had made up his mind and was free to follow it, gave up the policy of general toleration of all worships, and issued edicts ordering the observance of Sunday, prohibiting pagan rites (or at least such as he most disapproved), and granting some immunities and privileges to the Christian clergy.

Now though these changes must at any time have seemed most momentous, they were specially important in that they occurred at that moment. The Church was being convulsed by a great controversy.

The first duty incumbent on the Emperor when he adopted the new faith was to endeavour to restore unity to the Church.

The origin, significance, and results of the controversy are far too difficult for us to enter upon them now. I must merely note who the persons were that first raised the questions, and what evident and outward results followed. The difficulty began in Alexandria. That city, as you know, had been the meeting place of many ideas almost since its foundation, and of late had been the centre of an intellectual and theoretical form of Christianity. In the views maintained as to Christian doctrine, Alexandria was generally the rival of the Syrian city of Antioch. From Antioch came, apparently, the doctrines which made on this occasion so great a stir. They were held and proclaimed by a learned presbyter, or priest, named Arius. The great upholder of the contrary, the Alexandrian view, was a man of great ability and undaunted courage, Athanasius, afterwards Bishop of Alexandria, though only as yet chief adviser to the Bishop Alexander. The subject of the controversy cannot easily be put into a few words. I must, however, warn those whose chief association with the name of Athanasius is the creed commonly called after him, that no such connection really exists. The so-called Athanasian Creed originated in Western lands and at a much later date. The controversy was not exactly like any which has raged in our own times. There was no idea on either side of denying the Divinity of Christ, but the two sides interpreted that doctrine in different ways. Arius held that the Alexandrians, in their views as to the Incarnation of the Word of God, tended to become believers in two gods. Athanasius and his followers thought that any attempt to limit the eternity of Christ's being was an attack on His dignity.

It is difficult for us who have not Eastern minds, and generally care little for metaphysics, to understand how people should have become so intensely excited and have hated one another so much because of a difficult point in theology. When, however, the Bishop of Alexandria had excommunicated Arius and his followers, and they had consequently formed themselves into a sect, the question became one of law and order. Constantine, who was nothing of a scholar or a theologian, wrote a letter to the conflicting parties, full of common sense, but showing a blunt mind. It was of no good to tell the theologians that the various philosophical sects held various opinions and yet lived in peace together. To these eager partisans the questions were as of life and death. Then, especially as another question had arisen—that of the time at which men ought to keep Easter—the Emperor had recourse to another means, and called together all the bishops he could summon to meet in council. This first great Council was held at Nicæa in 325. More than three hundred bishops were there, and the Emperor presided in person, though he was at best but a new-fledged

Christian and had not even been baptised. The result was that a creed was drawn up to which all but four of the bishops present subscribed. It is almost, though not entirely, the same as the so-called Nicene Creed in the English prayer-book. But this did not end the matter. After a time, some of the bishops who had really sympathised with the Arians obtained the Emperor's ear, and obtained the recall of some of their friends. Athanasius, now Bishop of Alexandria, and very zealous for the creed of Nicæa, had most absurd charges brought against him. One was that he had cut off a man's hand, but this accusation was easily confuted, as the man in question, with both hands safe and sound, was unexpectedly produced at the Council of Tyre, which had to inquire into the affair. Other complaints were not so easily silenced. When the Emperor ordered him to receive back into the Church those who had followed Arius, he declared that to do so was against his conscience, and he was sent into banishment.

The strife was by no means over when Constantine died. Unfortunately it became very bitter among the barbarian nations who were shortly to spread all over the provinces of the Roman Empire. The Goths received Christianity from an Arian missionary, the Franks from those who accepted the Nicene or Catholic doctrine. Ultimately the cause of Athanasius prevailed, but that was not for many years, and meantime whichever side had the upper hand persecuted its opponents. It seemed as if the desire for sharing in the interests of the community, denied to men in matters of a political character, had found its vent in theological conflict, where it acted by means that we commonly regard as very unsuitable, and which *some* men saw to be unsuitable even then.

Constantine died in 357, at Nicomedia, whither he had gone to take a course of warm baths. He was baptised on his death-bed. The postponement of baptism till the last possible moment, frequently denounced by the chief Fathers of the Church, was due to the very severe penance imposed on all who committed any sins *after* baptism. As he lay dead, the attendants and courtiers who had waited on him still paid their respects with many bows and polite salutations, until the preparations for a magnificent funeral were complete.

He had ruled successfully on the whole, yet those last servile bowings before the imperial corpse seemed to betoken the hollowness and unreality of the world in which royal princes, such as he, commonly have to live. The Christian Church had risen to great success under his rule, had sprung from persecution to prominence. Yet was there not here, too, something of hollowness, as in the high-flown praises of the Christian Emperor by courtly bishops ? It may be so, yet neither Emperor nor bishops can here be regarded as responsible for the issues of their actions.

CHAPTER VII

THE GOTHS AND THE HUNS—ALARIC AND ATTILA

THE names at the head of this chapter will suggest to you that we are coming altogether to an end of Roman history properly so-called. They are names not of Romans but of barbarians. And as we have seen, old pagan Rome cannot be quite the same as before, now that the emperors have become Christians and while they dwell chiefly in a city far away to the East. But when we read a little more deeply into those times, we see that neither the conversion of Constantine nor the founding of Constantinople, nor even the destructive inroads of the barbarians, dethroned the Eternal City in the eyes of all men. We need only look at the kind of language used concerning her by prophets who denounced the evil in her and magnified her fall, and by the patriotic or courtly poets who refused to see, even after some of her worst misfortunes, that she had really sunk from her lofty seat, and we realise that as Rome was not built in a day, so many days were needed for her fall and her revival.

Meantime, we must feel some regret in bidding adieu to that ancient world which seemed to have contributed its best and its worst to make Rome what she had now come to be. We are leaving behind us " the brave days of old," of gods and heroes and heroic men, of noble poems and brilliant histories, of massive buildings for public business and for the worship of the nation's gods ; of statues and other works of art, fashioned it might be in imitation of Greek models, yet keeping up the memory of those masterpieces, and thus rendering an inestimable benefit to us who come after. Christian art and Christian life will yield yet nobler fruit in days to come, and Rome will again be the sea into which streams of thought and effort in art and letters and religion continually flow, but as yet there is a newness about the aspect of things without the freshness of youth. In Rome itself the temples were not destroyed, nor even the statues taken away all at once, even after pagan worship had been prohibited. As long as some pagans or half-pagans held the præfecture of the city of Rome, these were kept up. And we must not imagine that *all* the important people in Rome or in the Empire generally turned Christians with Constantine. A long time after, there was a hot dispute whether a statue of the goddess Victory should be allowed to keep its place in the Roman Senate House. But it was natural that people should care little for a symbol which had ceased to have sacred meanings for them, and should keep it negligently. Over some of the old temples, churches were erected, and material was occasionally removed from pagan to Christian buildings. The churches were not so imposing to look at as the old temples. They were built after the model of the law-courts, with a long body and a bay or apse at the east end. Thence the first churches were called *basilicas*, a name taken from the law-courts. They were often decorated with mosaic, and came to be enriched with costly gifts ; yet regarded as works of architecture, of course we could not compare them with the best of the Greek temples.

Meanwhile, in this pagan world which we are observing in its last stage, there was considerable appreciation of luxury without much discernment of beauty and good taste. There were plenty of people who could make grand-sounding speeches and write very long poems, and a few who could write charming letters, but not many who could write books worth reading except a few great men, like St. Augustine ; and their general attitude was unsympathetic not only towards the pagan or half-Christian life of their own times, but towards the forefathers whom they could not help imitating. There were rich nobles, in Rome and elsewhere, even when barbarians were hovering on the frontier and all the Empire was suffering from their ravages or from the taxes necessary to resist them. Men and women lived in ease and frivolity, and did not bestir themselves unless they had a rude awakening. The general decline in art of which I have spoken— the loss of power to discern clearly and to represent truthfully whatever by reason of its beauty or of our feeling for it needs to be represented—can be traced in melancholy fashion in the coins and medals dating from these centuries. The coins of Hadrian are delightful to look at. When we come to the coins of Diocletian and Constantine, we find still some striking portraits. The sons of Constantine are represented so that we cannot discern one from another. In a few more generations, the imperial coins are such that though we can see on them something evidently meant for a human face, we cannot in the least say what that face is supposed to be like.

The Romans of these days are unlike their predecessors, also, in fighting power. The most able generals in the period after Constantine have barbaric-sounding names, and the bravest troops consist of barbarian auxiliaries.

These considerations may console us as we turn away from the old pagan world. If we ask, "Whence is new life and strength to come, in order that the world may not go back to chaos or sleep away to death?" the answer is, "From the barbarians beyond the frontier."

This answer would have puzzled a real Roman of those days, to whom the idea of barbarism and of anarchy or chaos would naturally have gone together. Nor do we at the present time build much hope for the future on those peoples whom we regard as barbarous or uncivilised. Perhaps civilised societies are always apt to class the un-civilised all together, instead of observing that some are on the road to civilisation, others on the road back from a past greatness, and others can never be fit for any orderly mode of life. With us, the question of colour comes in. We are apt to set down as a " black man " the most intelligent of Hindoos and a cannibal from Polynesia. The Romans used the word *barbarous* to denote all nations that stood out-side the civilisation which belonged to themselves and the Greeks and those who had come under Roman and Greek influence. Their writers often made but slight distinctions between races that differed very much from one another. But as time went on, and barbarians became civilised enough to write the histories of their own people, and those who dwelt in the Roman provinces were forced into closer relations with them, differences in national character became very evident. And I think I may safely say that of the barbarian peoples who wrested most of Europe from the hands of the Romans, the two from which I have chosen the great leaders for us to look at now, stand at the very opposite ends of the scale in respect to capacity for appreciating and adopting a civilised life—the Goths come at the top of the ladder, the Huns at the bottom.

In your history books you will read about the

barbarian inroads which destroyed—to all practical intent—the whole Roman Empire. Of course you understand—though it is as well sometimes to recall to one's mind—that these inroads were very unlike a raid of savages on a modern European settlement. The wars were not generally wars of civilised men against savages. The soldiers in the Roman armies were in great part of barbarian extraction. And the barbarian hosts had often dwelt for years on the Roman frontier and learned a good deal of the ways of civilised life. The barbarians did not destroy the Empire at one fell swoop. They may rather be said to have gradually undermined the whole structure. Leading men among them obtained posts in court and army. Brave bands received the task of defending the frontier provinces. We can conceive that the whole face of things might have been changed gradually, without much fighting and destruction, if there had not been some movements among the peoples of the far East or the far North which pressed upon those who were nearer neighbours to the Romans, as melting snows force down avalanches into the valley. And, unfortunately, the frequent disputes among candidates for the imperial throne (as in the case of the six emperors we met with in our last reading) and the constant upstarting of usurpers, were always giving the barbarians a chance of seeing what opportunities lay open to them.

The barbarians of whom we read in the times of

the great inroads were for the most part great con-
federacies of tribes into which many of the tribes
we read of in earlier writers had become absorbed.
The Alamanni, who for a long time had their abodes
on the Rhine and frequently made expeditions into
Gaul, were a confederacy of this kind. So also
were the Vandals, who forced their way into Gaul
and afterwards into Spain, before they took up their
abode in Africa. So also were the Franks, with
whom we shall have much to do by and by. Most
of these people were Christians before they came to
the life-and-death struggle with the Roman provincials. But as most of them (though not the
Franks) had adopted the Arian form of Christianity,
and the Romans after Theodosius the Great were
almost all Catholic, there was not much religious
sympathy to soften the horrors of war.

At present, however, I wish to keep chiefly to the
story of one of these barbarian races, the Goths, of
their fightings and of their treaties with the Romans.
The dynasty of Constantine came to an end after the
death of his sons and his nephew. These were succeeded by two brothers, Valentinian and Valens, and
throughout the history of this period we have wars
carried on, sometimes successfully, sometimes the
reverse, between the Roman armies and the German
hosts on the Rhine and the Danube; also between
Romans and Persians in the valley of the Euphrates.
In the reign of Valens the whole State was alarmed
by the encroachments of the Goths. This people

had in far-back times inhabited the shores of the
Baltic. Before the end of the second century of
our era they had come down to the shores of the
Black Sea. I have already mentioned that in 251
they overthrew a Roman Emperor in battle. They
were a brave, capable race, tall and strong, and able
to appreciate the greatness of the Empire and to
learn from their enemy. They readily took to the
sea and sailed among the Greek cities of the Euxine
and the Ægean, spreading havoc as they went. At
length the province of Dacia, which, as you remember, was the chief conquest of the great Trajan,
was ceded to the western branch of them, the
Visigoths. The eastern branch, the Ostrogoths,
continued to inhabit the lands now belonging to
South Russia. During the time of peace which
followed, those nearest to the Romans were more or
less disciples of the Romans, though of course they
kept their own language. It is interesting to us that
the Goths, being a Germanic people, spoke a
language closely akin to Anglo-Saxon, so that even
now students of early English have to read the
Gothic translation of parts of the Bible made by the
missionary bishop Ulfilas. When wars and rebellions raged within the Empire the Goths were ready
to have their share in the fighting. They helped
Constantine against his last rival, Licinius, and in
the time of the brothers Valentinian and Valens
they wasted their energy in helping a usurper who
was soon overthrown.

But the great and serious attack on the Empire came after Valentinian had died, while his two young sons were ruling in the West and his brother Valens in the East. The cause of the disturbance should be sought, if we had to seek for it, far away in northern Asia, where the ball was set rolling which finally pressed down into Europe a race of savages such as the civilised-barbarian Goths regarded with horror. These were the Huns, a horde of hideous little men and women, with small bead-like eyes, misshapen faces, great skill in riding on ponies, but no inclination or capacity for cultivating the ground or following the arts of peace. They swooped down upon the Goths, overthrew for a time the kingdom of the Ostrogoths, and pressed upon the Visigoths in Dacia till they begged the Emperor to let them cross the Danube and settle in the lands on the other side. Valens granted this petition, but did not take measures for securing that his promises should be fulfilled. In his fear of the Goths, he ordered that their young sons should be taken from them and distributed through the cities of Asia Minor. The end of it all was that the Goths, half-starved, hopeless and indignant, joined with their new and loathsome foes, the Huns, against their late friends, the Romans. A great battle was fought at Hadrianople, a city dangerously near to Constantinople, in which Valens was killed—or perhaps he survived it to die a few hours or days later. The Emperors left were the two young sons of Valentinian, Gratian and Valentinian the Second. Now Gratian, a youth of about twenty, did the only wise thing to be done under the circumstances. He chose as colleague a brave and experienced man, Theodosius by name, a Spaniard—and thus a fellow-countryman of some of the great men of the Roman Empire.

Theodosius is remarkable chiefly for three things that he did. In the first place, he settled definitely the religious question, so far as the ruling authorities were concerned. He was baptised by a Catholic bishop, and allowed no credit and little freedom to the Arians. Secondly, he showed himself able to cope with the Goths in the hour of their victory and presumption. Not only did he save Constantinople from their ravages, but he made a peace with them by which they became allies, or confederates of Rome, with certain privileges of their own. Many served in his armies, and they showed an enthusiastic attachment to himself and his dynasty. The third act of Theodosius, an act the consequences of which he cannot possibly have foreseen, was the division of the Empire at his death.

Now this is a point that every one who wants to understand anything of European history ought to have quite clear in his mind. The year 395, that of the death of Theodosius, is a remarkable date, *not* because the Empire had never been divided before —there had been a similar division in the time of Diocletian, as we have seen, and another among the

sons of Constantine—nor yet that Theodosius con-
templated a real cutting of the Empire into two
quite separate states. He meant that there should
be two imperial residences, two courts, and to some
extent two sets of ministers. But neither he nor
any one else for centuries later would have thought
of two Empires, or even of one Empire so divided
that one part could not come to the help of the
other in case of need. The importance of the date
lies in the fact that owing to what we may call
accident (though this is a stupid word when used in
history, and is a mere confession of our own ignorance or laziness), from this time forth East and
West drifted apart and never really came together
again, for though we shall hear again of times when
there was only *one* Emperor, that one Emperor no
longer ruled over the whole with equal powers
similarly exercised in every part. Rivalries between
the courts, curious fancies in the minds of some
notable persons, differences in language and religion
which became more distinct as time went on, helped
to bring about this result. But I do not intend here
to inquire into the causes of the separation, only to
point out that after the death of Theodosius, the
countries ruled over in the East, by his son Arcadius,
were separated from those in the West, under
Honorius, by a line which goes through Illyria and
gives Macedon, Greece, and Egypt to the East, and
most of North Africa, with the chief countries
of modern Europe, to the West—a line roughly

answering to the twentieth meridian east of Greenwich.

There was a fourth thing that Theodosius did, for the results of which he was even less responsible than for those of the division of the Empire. He showed to Alaric, the Goth, the way into Italy. It came about on this fashion : the two young sons of Valentinian had short lives and tragic deaths. Theodosius, their brother-in-law and colleague, dealt very honourably with them, tried to prevent the fall of each in turn, and effectually avenged their deaths. On his expedition from the East into Italy, to chastise the tyrant or usurper who had been set up after the death of young Valentinian, he was accompanied by the young Gothic chieftain, whose name was to have a terrible sound to Italians for many generations.

We read of many noble, kingly characters among the Goths, and possibly if *one* strong dynasty of able men had ruled over East and West Goths alike during this critical part of their history, they might have bidden defiance to the Huns and need not have appealed for help to Rome. Generally, however, their chiefs acted without much agreement together or subordination to a higher authority. One splendid old Visigoth, Athanaric, the last of the pagans, made peace with Theodosius and came to Constantinople. When he saw the magnificence of the city, and all the order and power and the working-together of many men that is implied in

the spectacle of civilisation, he declared that the
Emperor was a god and no man, and that it was
presumptuous to lift hand against him. He died
soon after, and Theodosius honoured him with a
magnificent funeral and rode before his bier as
chief mourner.

Alaric was, though not a pagan, a man of somewhat the same type. He was of a noble family, but
apparently not made king till about the time of the
death of Theodosius. The German races generally
followed the excellent custom (when it would work)
of choosing men of special fitness, military and
other, as their kings, but always from one great
family that in itself commanded respect. As soon
as Alaric was made king, he persuaded his people
that the Goths had fought and laboured for others
long enough ; it was time for them to seek their own
interests. His plans were eagerly taken up, especially
now that the death of Theodosius had destroyed
the hope of a constant friendly and advantageous
agreement with the Empire. Alaric soon had at his
command a mighty host, and he led it first into the
land of Greece. He met with little resistance, chiefly
because the courts of East and West could not combine against him—in fact the chief minister of
Arcadius has been accused of first suggesting this
expedition to Alaric. But, according to the narra-
tive of those who could not learn to despise the
gods of Hellas, Athens had a stronger defence than
mortal men could provide. For Athene the Cham-

pion and the god-like Achilles appeared before the
presumptuous invader, and terrified him so that he
left the sacred city comparatively unspoiled.   He
gained, however, several important places in Greece,
and might probably have found a difficulty in making
his way back, as Stilicho, the greatest general of the
time, was marching against him, but the foolish court
of the East dreaded help from the West, and Stilicho
was forced to retire.   Alaric was accepted into some
kind of alliance with the court of Arcadius, and
obtained   authority   over   Illyricum.   He   soon
attempted an invasion of Italy, whither, as already
seen, he had once marched with Theodosius.   But
in these lands Stilicho could have his way for the
time, and the Goths were beaten in two battles, one
at Pollentia, near Turin, the other near Verona.
Most unfortunately for the Empire, Stilicho, a barbarian himself by birth, who had risen to greatness
and stirred jealousy in small minds, was soon after
this accused of treachery and put to death.

Now was Alaric's opportunity.   He always heard in
his ears, he said, the words ringing, "Thou shalt go
on into the City," and now there was no one to stand
in his way.   The Emperor Honorius, who certainly
would not have been of much use if present, had
celebrated a triumph in Rome for the victories of
Stilicho, and then retreated to his palace at Ravenna,
where he thought himself safer than he could be at
Milan.   It was a terrible time for Rome when the
Goths encompassed her and tried to starve her into

surrender. Embassies were useless : Alaric made a
jest of their offers : and the Emperor sent no help.
Could it be, thought some, that after all the change
in religion had been a mistake, and that Rome ought
to endeavour by some ancient sacred rites to recover
the protection of the Immortal Gods ? A public
sacrifice was prepared ; even Innocent, Bishop of
Rome, is said to have consented, " preferring the
safety of the City to his own opinion," as an admiring pagan historian says. But the rite was not celebrated. It seems as if the Senate might still have a
hankering after the old gods, while the people trusted
more to Christ and to St. Peter. In any case, nobody
seems to have opposed the melting down of the
statues of the gods, to complete the amount of gold
and silver which, with fabulous quantities of silk,
pepper, and other luxuries, Alaric consented to
accept for a ransom.

But he was soon to return again. He really seems
to have wished to make his work one of more than
mere destruction. He offered very moderate terms
to the Emperor. What he wanted was room and
provisions—an opportunity of making a permanent
settlement for his Goths. But bad advisers at
court thwarted even the most reasonable proposi-
tion, and before long came the news that Alaric had
penetrated into Rome, and instead of giving it up to
pillage, had set up a rival Emperor, Attalus by name,
formerly præfect of the City. This arrangement did
not last long. Alaric soon deposed the would-be

Emperor he had set up, and again negotiated with Honorius. Then in August, 410, came the really dreadful days for Rome, when Alaric for the third time made his way inside the walls and allowed pillage and firing where he had hitherto been anxious to spare. But according to the stories in Christian writers, St. Peter accomplished for at least the Church-property of Rome what Athene had done for Athens. On one occasion the mass of treasure, defended only by a woman, was solemnly escorted to a place of safety, when she declared to a Gothic soldier that it was the property of St. Peter. But it was not yet held that all Rome belonged to St. Peter and could look to him for succour as Athens had looked to her goddess.

Alaric did not long survive the siege of Rome. He departed after six days with the idea of conquering Sicily, and died after a short illness near the Straits of Messina. His brother-in-law, Adolf, led off the greater part of the Gothic host to Gaul and Spain. He married a sister of Honorius, and tried to live at peace with the Empire. He saw, he said, that it would be better to *restore* the Roman power by means of the Gothic valour, than to destroy a civilised power and set up a barbarous one in its place. Perhaps he did not entirely realise his views, but he shows us the Goths at their best ; *not to destroy but to invigorate* was their mission, and in part at least we shall see that they fulfilled it.

As to Honorius, he was less moved by the terrible

disaster to the great City than you or I have been. He cared little for Rome—just as some worthy people of our own day say they do not trouble themselves about politics or public affairs—but he cared a good deal about his chickens, and especially for a beautiful hen named Roma. Thus when one of his attendants came to him with the dreadful news, "Rome is destroyed!" he answered stupidly, "How can that be? She was feeding from my hand an hour ago!"

To English people these events have an interest in connection with our own history. Pretenders to the imperial throne were ready to spring up, more plentifully even in Britain than elsewhere. One of the usurpers—a really able man who for a time created a kind of western empire for himself and his son—withdrew a great part of the legions from Britain. More soldiers had to be withdrawn later, when Italy was trembling under the hand of Alaric. Meanwhile the Britons needed protection and defence more than ever. Not only had the wild Caledonians crossed the northern frontier; the seafaring Saxons had made destructive raids on the East Coast. But all their appeals to Rome were of no avail. They were advised to take measures for their own safety—and we all know the result.

Forty years after the death of Alaric, Rome had to face a far more formidable foe, the King of the Huns, whose dominion had been increasing at great strides since they had come into collision with the Goths, and set the avalanche sliding southwards.

AND CHILD. (*Probably Placidia and Valent*

Their kings only ruled directly over what we now call Hungary, with the neighbouring lands, but they held a kind of sovereignty over many tribes, German and other, and threatened to swoop upon Constantinople and do to it as Alaric had done to Rome. Meantime Rome, and especially her churches, had recovered some of the former wealth, as the imperial family and some of the nobles were not illiberal in gifts to holy places. Honorius had been, after a little war of succession, followed by his nephew Valentinian III. This boy was the son of Placidia, sister to Arcadius and Honorius, who had been in Rome when it was taken by Alaric, and after a brief captivity had married his brother-in-law Adolf, of whose friendliness with Rome we have already spoken. Unfortunately the rule of Adolf in the kingdom which he founded in Southern Gaul and Spain, under the supreme authority of the Emperor, was but short. He died, as did the little prince whom Placidia had borne to him, and the unfortunate lady, alone among strangers, led an anxious, adventurous life till she was able to return to Italy. There, however, she was treated with suspicion by her brother. She was married to a brave and experienced soldier, another Constantius, and became mother of a boy, Valentinian. The photograph opposite this page is of an ivory carving said to represent Placidia and her boy—in any case it gives an idea of the appearance of an imperial lady and child at this period, and shows that there are some exceptions to the rules I have laid down as to the utter decline of the arts at this time.

During the childhood of Valentinian III., Placidia was practically governor of the Empire in the West. But her troubles were not ended. The Huns and other formidable enemies were threatening all around. Happily, she had a very able though not always very faithful general, Aëtius, who proved himself a match even for the mighty Hunnish king, Attila. This Attila was the most powerful king of his race, an utter barbarian, with a natural longing to obtain access to the wealth and luxury of southern lands. He obtained an excuse from an unexpected quarter. Placidia had another child besides Valentinian, a daughter, Honoria, who had been impatient of the restrictions of court life, and at last became so troublesome that her mother was forced to send her to the court of her cousins at Constantinople, the son and daughters of Arcadius, who lived a very quiet and religious life. But Honoria had no inclination to their ways, and the wild thought entered her mind that she would offer herself in marriage to the great King of the Huns. Accordingly she sent him a bracelet and a promise of marriage—without stopping to inquire how many wives Attila had already. Now the King had a pretext for war, since he could demand the hand or at least the dowry of his bride from her relatives at Constantinople or Rome. It is needless to say that the betrothed were never married, probably they never saw one another. But the East had to buy a doubtful peace, and the West was overcome with horror as Attila, followed by numerous tribes of more or less barbarous warriors, threw himself upon the most flourishing provinces. The people who dreaded his savagery and felt that their sufferings had not been all undeserved, called him "the scourge of God," and he was pleased to adopt the title for himself.

In 451, the Huns invaded Gaul. Many stories were told afterwards of the terror they inspired, and of the encouragement which the people derived from the prayers and exhortations of the bishops, who are coming to be regarded as the natural protectors of their sees. At Orleans, the bishop kept the people at prayer in the churches, sending them from time to time to look out from the walls for the help that would assuredly come. He had been to the camp of Aëtius, to let him know of the needs of his people, though this he seems not to have told them. At Troyes, the bishop Lupus, by coming himself to Attila and working on his nobler or on his more superstitious feelings, persuaded him not to spoil the city. The greatest help that Aëtius obtained was an alliance with the Visigoths. Their king, Theodoric (not to be confounded with the greater Theodoric of whom we shall hear in our next reading), answered the appeal of the Emperor. A great battle was fought in the Catalaunian Plain, not far from the city of Troyes. Attila was beaten, and the result was to Gaul like the withdrawal of a terrible nightmare, though we must regret that the fine old Visigothic king fell in the battle.

Next year Attila was approaching the gates of Rome. On the way he had taken the city of Aquileia after a long siege, and some of the dwellers in the north-east corner of Italy had fled for refuge to the islands and low ground at the mouth of the Po. This was the beginning of the city of Venice, though her day of glory was yet to come. Thence Attila came on to Milan and established himself in the palace. But in Rome he had a yet more powerful opponent than Aëtius—Leo the bishop, or pope. This great champion of his flock played a very different part from that of Innocent in the siege by Alaric. He went out bravely with an embassy to meet the invading host in Lombardy, perhaps at the confluence of the Mincio and the Po, and persuaded Attila to withdraw, on receiving the "dowry" which he claimed. It was said that Attila saw beside Leo the figure of St. Peter, admonishing him to give heed to the bishop's words. However that may be, Attila withdrew, and Rome was not sacked by the Huns. Shortly afterwards he took another wife, and was found dead, with her sitting by his side, after the bridal banquet. With him the greatest days of the Huns had come to an end.

Thus the Goths had aimed at a renewal, the Huns at the destruction of the Empire. Yet, as things were, the Goths must needs sometimes destroy, the Huns prepare the renewal. Alaric, in despite of Athene and of St. Peter, had carried away wealth from Athens and from Rome. Attila practically acknowledged the power of spirit over brute force when he turned aside and spared the City.

CHAPTER VIII

THEODORIC THE GOTHIC KING AND JUSTINIAN THE EMPEROR

WE should indeed want sharp eyes and clear heads to make out the course of the procession now passing before us. It is a strange medley. Men of many races, lawful rulers, assassins, champions of the people, jostle against one another as they pass by, few, if any, knowing whither they are bound. There are notable figures standing above the confused crowd, some of them visible from the city of Rome, others from more westerly or more easterly points of view. Very few of these greater men wear the imperial diadem. Some are strong, well-knit barbarians, generally clad in Roman dress. Others wear the bishop's mitre, and these seem to be hurrying to and fro seeking to save the lives of prisoners or to induce proud conquerors to think of peace. Great havoc and destruction is wrought in the unseemly struggles, and our eyes dwell most willingly on those who, whether for a longer or a shorter time,

132

spread around them the reign of law and order, and who, even if they are not able themselves to over-come the violence of their age, may help those that come after them to care for civilisation with all that it means, and to labour for its restoration.

A notable year in the history of Rome and of the world is 476 A.D.—about twenty-three years after the death of Attila the Hun. Long before this time, the dynasty of the great-hearted Theodosius and of the chicken-hearted Honorius had come to an end. One emperor after another had enjoyed, or at least possessed, the imperial honour for a short time. One had owed his position to the friendliness of the Visigoths in Spain, others to the emperors ruling at Constantinople ; another, strange to say, to the Vandals in Africa. These barbarians were, for a short time, very powerful in changing the fortunes of great countries. They nearly got a hold on Italy at one time, thanks to a lady who played much the same part in the wars of the Vandals as Honoria had taken in the invasion of Attila.

This lady was the widow of the Emperor Valentinian III., the son of Placidia. He had come to a very disgraceful end. Being a little-minded man, he was jealous of the great general Aëtius, who had saved Europe from the Huns. He accordingly sent for the general, on pretence of wanting some talk with him, and then foully stabbed him, not, you may be sure, without the help of some of his own officials, who could make sure of his work. Very soon afterwards, Valentinian was stabbed in revenge by some friends and followers of Aëtius, and a Roman noble of birth was set on his throne. The late Emperor's widow, Eudoxia, was his cousin, coming of the family that dwelt at Constantinople. The new Emperor, suspected of having plotted her husband's death, demanded her hand in marriage. All the women of the Theodosian house seem to have had great spirit, love of power, and susceptibility to injury or insult, with very little care for the public good. Eudoxia appealed to the King of the Vandals. Again a great barbarian host appeared before Rome. Again the city was sacked, though again the good bishop Leo kept things from coming to the worst. The Vandals did not keep Rome. Eudoxia and her daughter were among the prisoners they carried back to Africa. One of the prisoners was married to a Vandal prince. The other became the wife of an emperor who ruled a short time under Vandal patronage.

None of these emperors, however, were important persons. The *person* of importance, whether Roman or barbarian, was whosoever could control the bands of auxiliaries, or hired soldiers, chiefly of barbarian race, who had gradually been flocking into Italy from beyond the Alps, and enlisting in the legions. For about sixteen years, one man, half-Goth, half-

Sueve, pulled down and set up emperors as he pleased, bearing the title of *Patrician*, which, you see, had entirely lost its old meaning. When he fell, another "patrician," Orestes, a Roman provincial by birth, took the same title and secured the imperial dignity for his young son, Romulus Augustulus. It seemed afterwards a sad jest that the last emperor who ruled from Rome should bear the names of the first king and the first emperor with a slight addition to betoken how much slighter a creature was he than they. For his reign (if we may so call it) is marked by the event of 476, which, as I have said, is an important one to know. This event is nothing less than the bringing to an end of the Roman Empire in the earliest Roman lands. But here we must remember that this by no means brought with it the extinction of the Roman Empire, for there was still an emperor at New Rome, or Constantinople ; and also that the days were to come when Rome would again see emperors crowned within her sacred walls. But that was not to be till after many attempts and disappointments, and the rise and fall of great nations.

How things came about was briefly thus : the barbarian forces mutinied, and tried to force Orestes to give one-third of the lands of Italy into their possession. Orestes refused, and they chose for their champion a fine, tall barbarian, named Odoacer. We cannot feel quite certain as to his nation, though we gather that he was some kind of German. He was made king, and Orestes took refuge in Pavia. But the city was soon taken and the Patrician put to death. Odoacer was now the most powerful man in Italy, and over his followers he reigned as *king*. But to the rest of the Italians he was no king, nor did he exercise over them any lawful authority. People still regarded the Emperor as the source of such authority. The pretty boy whom Orestes had set on the throne had given up his position, and was thankful to be allowed to live in a beautiful seaside house near to Naples. If Odoacer wanted to seem better than a mere usurper, it was to Constantinople that he must look for sanction of his extraordinary powers.

The Emperor at this time was Zeno. He was not a man of great ability or distinction of any kind, and had lately been fighting for his throne against his wife's uncle. The honour of being appealed to by the Western lands must have flattered his vanity, though it did not mean much that was serious. The Senate of Rome sent him an embassy bearing some of the symbols of imperial rule (" ornaments of the palace," they were called)—probably a diadem and a purple robe—and assured him that henceforth one emperor would be sufficient, and that they would like to be under him. They asked him, accordingly, to bestow the title of *Patrician* on Odoacer, that he might, under the Emperor, defend and rule the land of Italy.

Now it was not easy for the Emperor to do *exactly* as was wished, because one of the emperors lately deposed, and now living in banishment, had originally come from Constantinople and was related to Zeno's wife. Zeno did not take a very decided line. He wrote a kind letter to the banished Emperor Nepos (of the poor little Augustulus he seems to have taken no notice). He advised the senators to recall Nepos, and to ask him to give the patriciate to Odoacer. But, at the same time, he intimated that he was not unwilling to grant the title, and in fact he actually wrote a letter addressed, " To Odoacer the Patrician." Needless to say, the diadem did not find its way back at present. So henceforth, for twelve or thirteen years, Odoacer, King and Patrician, ruled over Romans and barbarians in Italy. But we must notice that he was still only *king* to his own people. Though a much more powerful man than Zeno, he preferred to seem to the Italians a mere subordinate of the Emperor. He ruled not unwisely on the whole, using the services of men who knew Roman ways and Roman law, and carrying on war, at times, with barbarous tribes to the north. At first he lived on better terms with Zeno than one might have thought possible, seeing that he was a barbarian adventurer, and Zeno was regarded as universal ruler. But, in course of time, difficulties arose between them. I cannot go into them now ; indeed, historians are not all of one mind as to what the difficulties exactly were. Some of them seem to have been connected with a quarrel between the Pope of Rome and the Patriarch of Constantinople, for religious differences counted for very much in those days. However it may have been, Zeno came to wish that Odoacer were not in Italy, and that another and more dangerous man were there rather than at his own court. And these wishes brought about the coming into Italy of Theodoric the Ostrogoth.

We saw in our last reading how the great people of the Goths had gradually pressed nearer to Roman lands until they threatened the City itself. We saw also how they had split into two branches, one of which, the Visigoths, afterwards settled in Gaul and Spain, and helped the Romans against the Huns. The other branch, the Ostrogoths, dwelt for a long time in the regions to the north and east of Italy, and were obliged for a while to acknowledge the Huns as their masters. But in time their power revived, and they threw off the yoke. At this time they were under the rule of three valiant brothers, Walamir, Theodemir and Widemir. On the very day of a great victory of the Goths over the Huns, a son was born to the second brother, Theodemir, who called his name Theodoric.

These Ostrogothic brothers were sometimes useful but always formidable neighbours to the emperors

that dwelt at Constantinople. To make sure of their
fidelity, the Emperor demanded, when Theodoric
had reached the age of seven years, that the boy
should be sent as hostage to Constantinople and
brought up there. In Constantinople, accordingly,
he spent the next ten years of his life, under the eye
of the Emperor Leo. What kind of education he
received we cannot tell. He did not acquire much
book learning; indeed one of his biographers says that
he never knew how to write. But he learned one
thing: that civilisation, even such as prevailed under
the Eastern emperors, was better than barbarism
with all its lawless freedom. At the age of seventeen,
he returned to his kinsfolk, and soon distinguished
himself in their wars with neighbouring tribes. In
a few years his father died, and he became King,
and took upon himself the responsibility of providing
his great host of warriors, and their wives and
children, with food and clothing in desolate and
wasted lands, and of meeting the crafty policy of
imperial statesmen and the rivalry of jealous chief-
tains among his own people. We cannot stop now
to trace his fortunes during this part of his life. His
name is not preserved untarnished. He was not
always straightforward in his dealings—but he was
sorely provoked to deceit. He allowed the blood of
his own Goths to be shed in disputes among themselves or in contests between rival emperors. He on
one occasion made away with one of his own kinsmen in order to satisfy the Emperor. But in judging

of his character, we must remember that though treachery and murder always have been and always will be treachery and murder, and though Theodoric, being an admirer of civilisation and a Christian as well, would never have denied that treachery and murder are wrong, yet those days of violence had made men very regardless of the worth of human life, and big-made men like Theodoric must feel the task of self-restraint all the harder because they have such strong selves to restrain. However this may be, the time came when Theodoric realised that though he might enjoy the honour of Consul, and shine among the great officers of the imperial court, yet his chief duty was to his own people. He knew that the Emperor Zeno disliked the rule of Odoacer in Italy. Accordingly he asked and obtained permission to lead his people into Italy, to take possession of the land and to rule it under the Emperor, whom he called his master and father.

It was a hard task indeed that he now had before him. It was not an army, but a nation that had to be transported into Italy, with women (among them Theodoric's mother), children, flocks and herds. Then Odoacer himself did not give way without five years of fighting. At last Ravenna was taken, and Odoacer, who had taken refuge there, made terms with the conqueror. Now Theodoric's worst side again showed itself. He was angry with the rival king because of treacherous acts against some of his friends, and to avenge them he became guilty of a baser treachery still, by hewing down the old man with his own hand at a banquet.

Yet after this hateful deed, Theodoric set to work to accomplish a truly noble task, the establishment of a kingdom, taking in all Italy and some lands to the west and north, in which Romans and Goths, Catholics and Arians, Christians and Jews, might dwell in peace together, obeying the law (not the same *laws* for all), and reverencing the King and the shadowy Emperor in whose name he ruled.

He had able men to help him, and in general he knew how to use their services. Most of what we know about his laws and his undertakings comes to us from the letters of a very worthy but rather long-winded secretary, a native of South Italy. As this man was exceedingly different from the Gothic King in every possible way, except in love of good order and strong government, the letters are not exactly what they would have been if written or dictated by Theodoric himself. But at least they make us understand what a watchful care the King exercised over all parts of the land over which he ruled ;—how he appointed governors and judges with Roman titles to see that justice was done among the Romans, and Goths, with barbarous-sounding titles, to keep down the high spirit of the Goths. "We view all our subjects," says one letter, "with an impartial love ; but he may commend himself more abundantly to our favour who controls his will and cleaves to the law." Again and again he exhorts all

who hold office to do what is just without respect of
persons or nations.   He issued a kind of code of
his own, drawn from Roman laws, to fill up what
was lacking in the customs of the Goths.   Nor did
he merely keep the kingdom at peace.   He loved to
beautify the great towns, especially Ravenna, still
the chief seat of the court, where a church built by
him, and adorned with fine mosaics, is still standing,
as well as his own great tomb.   He visited Rome, to
pray in the church of St. Peter, to delight the people
with shows, and to undertake useful works, such as
the draining of the marshes.   One of the things
most to his credit is the impartial way in which he
behaved towards men of different religious principles.
He was himself an Arian, though his mother was a
Catholic, but he seems to have wished to insist more
on the things as to which Christians are agreed than
on those about which they differ.   Thus he remained
on good terms with many of the leading Catholics,
and he was able to settle the disputed election of a
Pope of Rome.   He showed his justice and good
sense in dealing with the Jews, who suffered cruel
persecutions at the hands of most Christians at this
time, and were hated with mad fury by the people
generally.   In fact Theodoric saw, and stated clearly
in the orders he gave concerning them, that "no man
can be compelled to believe."   Of course he thought
his own belief the best, and he had a care for orderly
worship in noble buildings.   But he stands above
most men of his own and of succeeding ages in

having understood the need, for a well-ordered state, of as much religious toleration as can be borne at the time.

It was not only within the realm of Italy that the name of Theodoric was honoured and feared. When we read of the alliances he made, and the influence he exerted, by marrying his daughters and his near relatives to the kings of various nations, we seem to be looking at the foreign policy of some great sovereign of a much later date. His sister was married to a King of the Vandals, and her daughter, niece to Theodoric, became wife of a Thuringian King. The two elder daughters of Theodoric were married one to a King of the Burgundians, the other to a King of the Visigoths in Spain. His own second marriage was to a sister of the great King of the Franks, Clovis, and his daughter by this marriage was regarded by him as his heiress (most unluckily he had no son) and married to one of her own people. The Franks were afterwards to play a great part in the history of Italy, and of all Europe, but before Clovis they did not penetrate far into Gaul, which was in great part subject to Visigoths and Burgundians. Clovis was the first of the Frankish Kings to become a Christian, and the form of Christianity which he and his Franks adopted was the Catholic, not the Arian, professed by most of the barbarian nations. We shall see that this was of very great importance afterwards in making the Roman provincials and the Popes of Rome look to them rather than to others for succour and protection in time of need. Now the Frankish power was the rising one in those days, and both Visigoths and Burgundians were drawn into wars with Clovis and his sons. Here we see the opportunity given to the great Theodoric to intervene in their affairs. When Clovis made war on the Visigoths, and slew the King, Theodoric's son-in-law, in battle, Theodoric upheld the cause of the heir, his little grandson, and for a time ruled over a part of Spain as his guardian. When the Franks seemed likely to overthrow the kingdom of the Burgundians, Theodoric helped his allies to continue a little while longer. He had good generals, and was not slow to take the field himself, when necessary; but abroad, as at home, he preferred peace and order to strife and confusion, and his letters to his friends and kinsmen were in favour of agreement and moderation.

But how were these doings of Theodoric viewed by the Emperors in the East? On the whole, till the last bad years of the King's reign, the Emperor seems not to have had much cause for quarrel. Theodoric was master, indeed, but he was too strong to want to insist on his strength. On his coins he stamped the image of the Emperor, not his own. And though we hear that the "ornaments of the Palace," sent to Constantinople after the deposition of Augustulus, were sent back to Theodoric, we do not find him ever setting himself up as Emperor of the Romans.

At last, however, after more than thirty years of strict and righteous rule, events occurred which, though we do not and probably never shall know their exact order and meaning, have cast a gloomy and lurid light, like a stormy sunset, over the last days of Theodoric. He seems to have committed both crimes and mistakes that we should not have expected from him. According to one account, he set about persecuting the Catholics, and sent the Pope of Rome on a mission to the Emperor, to obtain unreasonably high terms for the Arians. The Emperor (Justin was ruling now) had taken to persecuting this sect, and it may be that Theodoric intended to liberate those who held his own form of faith by retaliating on the adverse party. Whatever his motives were, his policy failed. Pope John was well received in the East, but on his return, Theodoric showed great wrath against him and threw him into a prison, where he fell sick and died.

Nor was Theodoric in his later days more happy in his relations with the Roman senators and the ministers whom he had hitherto honoured and trusted. Some of them seem to have been corresponding with the Emperor, in the hope of putting an end to the Gothic rule. But none had a fair trial, and it is probable that some were imprisoned and put to death who were guilty of no crime. One of them, the philosopher Boethius, wrote in his captivity of the "Consolations of Philosophy," and his book is one to which many people of later days

have looked for thoughts to help them in bearing
patiently the evils that befall even the most righteous
of men.   It is said that the death of Theodoric was
hastened by his remorse for his violent deeds.   Had
he, too, after so long a schooling, failed to realise
the need of moderation in the use of supreme
power ?

After the death of Theodoric, a most saddening
chapter in history opens before us. The Gothic
kingdom seemed the one hope for the strong and
peaceable union of the wisdom of the old world
with the vigour of the new.   A few years, and this
hope collapsed utterly.   Theodoric's son-in-law had
died before him, leaving a young son, Athalaric.
This boy was being carefully brought up by his
mother, Amalasuntha, who had the same respect as
her father had for ancient civilisation, but thought
perhaps more than he did of the intellectual culture
which it implied.   In any case, she insisted on the
boy's being taught literature.   The Gothic nobles
were afraid lest he should turn into a bookworm.
They quoted a saying of Theodoric that "a boy
who fears the rod will never despise the sword."
Amalasuntha gave way.   But Athalaric was one of
those natures that need the rod.   The discipline of
the camp might have been as good for him as the
discipline of the schoolroom.   Being subject to
neither, he gave himself up to self-indulgence,
ruined his constitution, and died without attaining
full manhood. Meanwhile, Amalasuntha had secured

first the banishment, then the death, of the Gothic nobles who had withstood her. She sent to a kinsman to share the throne with her. He played her false, stirred up strife against her, and finally caused her to be murdered.

A more notable Emperor was now ruling in the East, Justinian, nephew of Justin. He was not a man of first-rate ability, but he had rare opportunities and he used them cleverly. Amalasuntha had appealed to him. He proposed conditions to her successor which were humiliating to the Goths. The result was a long and terrible war ending in the downfall of the Gothic kingdom. The imperial victories were due chiefly to the great ability of the general sent by Justinian, Belisarius. His was a life of much glory and much suffering, through the jealousy of his rivals and the want of confidence shown by the Emperor. At one time, after Belisarius had been recalled and a gallant young Goth had been chosen king, it seemed as if the tables must be turned. The Goths recovered Rome, which had stood two long sieges. But in the end, the generals of Justinian prevailed, the Goths were ordered to withdraw from Italy, and for a time the land was again directly subject to the Emperor who ruled at Constantinople.

The City of Rome had suffered terribly from the great sieges she had had to undergo during the Gothic war. It is, however, not Rome but Ravenna that was the seat of the Gothic monarchy and afterwards of the governor sent from Constantinople. Yet the Goths realised the importance of the City, and the struggles of the Popes against the Bishops of Constantinople, though not always ending triumphantly for Rome, kept her claims before men's eyes.

The name of Justinian is associated with other great works besides the reconquest of Italy. It was he who ordered the formation of the Roman Law into a Code, which has been of inestimable importance in the study of Law and in practical lawmaking from that day onwards. For Justinian was as well served by his great lawyers as by his great generals. He also built one of the most famous churches in the world, St. Sophia, now used as a Turkish mosque. And though we find a difficulty in keeping in mind his connection with *Rome*, we must look on him as one of the emperors who vindicated the honour of Roman arms and asserted the majesty of Roman Law.

Meantime, how had all these contests affected the state of the Roman Church, the head of which had sometimes of late represented the greatness of the Roman name even more than the Emperor himself? The ecclesiastical headship of the world became for a time somewhat obscured. There were two unfortunate facts which prevented the Bishops of Rome from doing all that might have been done to prevent or to soften the horrors of war and to keep up the order which Theodoric had laboured to establish. One fact was that neither the popes nor the clergy generally could quite forget that, after all, Theodoric was to them a heretic, and that the Gothic rule, if respected, could never be loved. The other was that a great rivalry and dissension had sprung up between the churches of the East and the West. It was not for a long time yet that the great breach occurred which separated the Greek Church from the Roman. But even now, men were ready to make the most of small or incomprehensible differences in doctrine, and bitter personal differences as to the worthiness or unworthiness of rival fathers and bishops, so that the unity of the Church seemed to have become even less real than the unity of the Empire. For a time after the expulsion of the Goths, the Popes are unimportant persons, looking to Constantinople for assistance against the adversaries whom they have next to encounter. The great City had lost not only her finest buildings, but the bountiful supply of water which had been her boast for centuries. Yet there were men to come who should render her more venerated than ever before, and make her such a head and rallying centre as she would never have been under Theodoric. And these men were to arise not from subtle Eastern Emperors, nor from brave Gothic kings, but from the bishops and clergy of the City of Rome.

CHAPTER IX

RENEWAL OF THE EMPIRE IN ROME

THE end of our last chapter was rather dis-
heartening. We might have called that whole
chapter the story of a great opportunity missed.
Now we pass on, through some centuries of violence
and disorder, to the story of a great opportunity
taken. What had been lost was the prospect of a
well-ordered Italian kingdom, retaining much of
what was best in ancient civilisation, and opposing
a barrier to the inroads of barbarous and destructive
peoples into the lands where there was still some
care for learning, for beauty, and for peaceful and
social life. What was afterwards gained was the
restoration, in Rome herself, of an Empire that
again claimed the right to rule over the whole
civilised world, the power being once more placed
in hands that were fit to use it. We shall see, in
time, that the restoration, or renewal, of the Empire
with Rome for its centre, did not, in practice, bring
about all that was hoped from it. Nor, perhaps, had

the attempt of Theodoric been as futile as it seemed on the day when the Goths promised to depart from Italy, for even the memory of his work may have borne some fruit later. *Success* and *failure* are words to be used only in a comparative sense, in historical matters, as we have said before. But we must return to our post of survey, and see how things appeared from Rome in the middle of the sixth century after Christ.

You remember that when the Goths left Italy, the whole country was supposed to have come back under the dominion of the Emperor who lived at Constantinople, whose supreme authority had been acknowledged even by Theodoric, though he had a fairly free hand in the lands he had conquered from Odoacer and others. Now, the Emperor ruled by means of a deputy called the Exarch, whose residence was at Ravenna, where, you remember, Theodoric had generally dwelt, and some of the emperors before his time. If there were any people then alive who had been observing the course of events, and who were not too intensely interested in what was near at hand to feel some curiosity as to the future, we can imagine that the question would arise in their minds : How long can this arrangement last ?

Let us suppose that we can get hold of such a spectator of events, a descendant, about six generations down, of the clever man whose opinions we asked as to the coming changes in Constantine's time. I can imagine that he might say : "The probability of things going on smoothly under present arrangements depends on several questions ; one is, will any more barbarians from the North press in to fill the space left by the Goths ? Another is : will the Emperors at Constantinople have time to attend to matters in these parts, or will they have wars and dangers on their Eastern borders, so that they have to keep their thoughts fixed on other enterprises ? And above all, how will these Emperors get on with the Bishops of Rome—the Popes as you call them ? Those ' Bishops are not of very much account just now, but they are likely to become more important after the heretics are gone ; and after all, they are of more weight than anybody else in the City. The Senate need not concern us much. It may set up pretensions from time to time, and it may have champions, but it will not be of much account any more. That is how things stand. If the Popes and Emperors hold together, and there are no more barbarian invasions, all may go well. But if there are barbarians—not like Theodoric's Goths, but untamed men who care little either for Emperor or Pope, and if there are any more bitter quarrels—as there are likely enough to be between East and West as to religion or government, or anything else—then I see little hope for Rome or Italy, and none at all for the cause of law and order."

To our imaginary spectator, those of us who know

some history would reply that other and fiercer barbarians from the North would shortly swoop down on Italy; that the Emperors of the East would find themselves exposed to greater dangers and would suffer far more serious losses in the East within about seventy years than ever before ; and that in the midst of the troubles, serious religious differences would again arise between East and West, so that Constantinople and Rome would come to look upon one another with no friendly eyes.   But as to his loss of hope for Rome and for civilisation, we should add that at least a partial renewal of the glories of the Roman Empire was to come from a nation of barbarians lately settled in Gaul, whose name had been a byword for faithlessness and cruelty among both Romans and Goths.   At this he could but shrug his shoulders and say, "This is a strange world.   We cannot, any of us, see far ahead," and so leave us to look a little closer at the facts we have been setting before him.

First, as to the fierce barbarians who invaded Italy after the Goths had retired.   These were the Lombards, who had long ago come south, like other Germanic peoples, from the shores of the Baltic, had been allowed to fight the battles of the Romans, and had, in reward, received grants of land on the border.   They seem to have been more wild and fierce than those who had invaded Italy before them.   The Exarchs at Ravenna and the Popes of Rome could find no words bad enough for them, and perhaps they were all the more likely to plunder and pillage everywhere in that, unlike Odoacer and Theodoric and those who came with them, they had no title or authority to justify their invasion.   People who like to attribute any great evil to some particular person, if possible to a woman, told a story afterwards how the Empress Sophia at Constantinople had insulted the great general Narses at Ravenna, and how he in revenge called in the Lombards, as Honoria had summoned the Huns and Eudoxia the Vandals.   But this story is by no means probable.   In any case, the Lombards acted on their own account, though accompanied by a good many other tribes as uncivilised as themselves. In religion they were Arians, but more given, as yet, to destroying the churches of the Catholics than to building new ones of their own.   Their rough and barbarous ways are shown in the death of the king who had led them into Italy, Alboin.   In his youth he had fought against a neighbouring tribe, the Gepids, and slain one of their princes, in spite of which the Gepid king bestowed on him his arms (knighted him, we should have said in later times) and showed him bounteous hospitality.   Later, another Gepid war arose, and Alboin slew Cunimand, the successor of the hospitable king. He then took his daughter to wife.   A sad fortune for the lady, we are inclined to say, but we are approaching the age of chivalry, in which, in the

words of a fine Spanish ballad, a knight might
say :

" I slew a man, I owe a man ; fair lady, by God's grace
 An honoured husband shalt thou have in thy dead father's
  place."

But Alboin was not perfectly chivalrous, at least
not after his drinking bouts, nor was Rosamund a
perfectly submissive wife. One night, being heated
with wine, the King sent Rosamund his drinking-
cup, made of the skull of her father, and adorned
with gold and pearls. The Queen drank and made
no complaint. But not many days after, Alboin
went to his wife's apartment for his midday sleep,
and as he lay, the Queen opened the door to the
assassins whom she had won over. The King felt
for his sword, but Rosamund had removed it. He
withstood his enemies by seizing a stool as a weapon
of defence or attack, but this resistance could not
last long. Fierce ruffian as he was, he was lamented
by his soldiers.

Not *all* the Lombard kings were as fierce as
Alboin. Nor were all of them great conquerors.
The conquest of Italy by the Lombards occupied
many years. In fact it never was quite finished.
Ravenna, where the Exarch from Constantinople
lived, and Rome, where the Popes and the people
still thought they held " the headship of the world,"
managed generally to keep the Lombards aloof,
and to keep up some communication with one

another, though once or twice the Lombards seized towns on the road which ran between them. Then not all even of the part of Italy which the Lombards had conquered was subject to the Lombard king who ruled at Pavia. There were two large duchies more to the south, the rulers of which were sometimes more dangerous to the Popes than were the kings themselves. In justice to the Lombards, we should here say that though fierce and violent, they were not incapable of appreciating the blessings of peace and order. When they were well settled down, they put their laws into writing, and though the laws have a barbarous look (they prescribe that you must pay six shillings to a man if you cut off his great toe, and only three shillings if you cut off his little toe) yet they are better than no laws at all. There was one lady who seems to have had a good deal of influence in softening and taming the wild fierceness of the Lombards. This was Theudelinda, the Bavarian, who was married to one Lombard king, and on his death to another, for her second husband was chosen as successor by the Lombards so that they might still have Theudelinda for their Queen. She was a Catholic in religion, and her son was baptised into the same faith. She was on friendly terms with one of the best of the Popes, Gregory the Great, who looked to her for help in his strivings after peace. But though some of the Lombards might be regarded as right in their beliefs, and as people with whom it was worth while to be on good terms, yet neither Popes nor Emperors loved them, but agreed (though they might agree about hardly anything else) in wishing that the Lombards were not there.

But how about the Emperors? You remember how our intelligent spectator considered it a question of great importance whether or no they would have any difficulties in the East to distract them in their attention to the West, and I hinted that the dangers ahead in that direction were very serious indeed.

In the first place, they had the same powerful enemy against whom they had done much hard fighting during many years, the King of Persia. His men were barbarians, likewise, especially the almost savage Avars, who dealt the Romans many hard blows. But early in the seventh century, an Emperor of real ability and courage retrieved the glory of the Roman name (notice that the Empire and those who belong to it are still always *called* Romans) and won back the provinces of Egypt and Syria, which the Persians had torn from the Empire. This included the recovery of the True Cross, which had fallen into the hands of non-Christians. But just as the sky seemed to be clearing, a great storm broke forth from a new and unexpected quarter.

The year 622 still marks the period from which many millions of men date their era. In that year a man about forty years old took flight from his own city, Mecca in Arabia, because he had proclaimed a religious doctrine which his fellow-citizens could not receive, and took up his abode in Medina, also an Arabian city, where he was able to attract more followers and to lay down laws for their guidance. The man's name was Mahomet, and the message he had to declare was that "There is no God but God," almighty and all-merciful; that all men return to God and have to give account to Him; and that the will of God as to the duties of man had been revealed to Mahomet, who was His Prophet.

But how can an event of this sort concern us and our questions about Emperors and Popes and Barbarians and the City of Rome? Arabia has always seemed far enough away from the Middle of the World, and the Arabs have never before this taken a great place in history. Besides, these doctrines do not sound so very new. The Christians, and the Jews before them, believed in One God and in judgment to come, and though they do not believe in Mahomet as a prophet, they have in their own sacred books much teaching about life and duty which cannot be *altogether* different from what Mahomet taught. True, but the rise of a new religion is one of the things that are impossible for us to foretell or to explain. Somehow or other, Mahomet made people really believe in his teaching and his mission, so that all other things, quiet and ease, wealth, life itself, seemed as nothing in comparison with the duty of spreading the faith, and the joys that await the faithful hereafter. Then—

important for us to notice—Mahometanism, unlike Christianity, was a religion of the sword. Christians have fought for their faith, of course, either to keep it for themselves or to force it on others, but fighting is not and cannot be looked upon as the right and ordinary means of spreading the Christian religion. With Islam, the religion of Mahomet, fighting the enemies of the faith was from almost the first regarded as the noblest kind of work. And the enemies of the faith were, of course, the subjects of the Emperor. Mahomet himself sent messages to the Emperor, and to the King of Persia, bidding them to accept Islam. They were not likely to do so, but the Christianity of the Eastern provinces was not strong enough to make a firm stand. As we have already seen, people had wasted their strength and lost all feeling of a common Christianity through useless disputes on very difficult theological questions. And again, strange as it may seem to us, Christianity was everywhere putting on a form likely to exasperate those whose great idea was that there is but one God. Sacred symbols, pictures and relics, and such things, were venerated by everybody, and made into idols by ignorant people. Though men believed in God the Father, He seemed so far off that they preferred to approach Him through the saints, who had been men of human feelings, and at whose tombs or shrines, as everybody believed, miracles were still continually wrought. But whether through want of religion, or through want of patriotism, or from whatever cause, when the successor of Mahomet in his government, the Caliph Abu-Bekr, led or sent large and enthusiastic armies into Syria and into Egypt, the Imperial power collapsed utterly. Great cities like Damascus and Antioch, and the holy city of Jerusalem, were taken one after the other. Not only what was most sacred and ancient, but also what was most useful to the Emperors, was lost for ever, since Egypt had been from of old the corn-growing country for Mediterranean lands. Before long, the Moors of Africa had been compelled to accept the new religion. Still more threatening to Christendom was the conquest of Spain by the Mahometans, which took place about seventy years later, when the Saracens (or Arabs) were invited in by a treacherous general of the Visigoths. It might seem as if Islam were about to supersede Christianity everywhere. We shall see how Christian champions were among the people that renewed the Roman Empire. But in all our readings of history for many centuries, we must bear in mind that brave and fierce Mahometan races—first Arab, then Turk— were *always* threatening the Christian world, and often seizing a province from the hands of the Emperor who ruled at Constantinople, or from the governors of the West.

So much, then, for the inroads and conquests of northern barbarians and for the troubles of the Emperors in their eastern territories. Now let us inquire into the other question asked us : how the Eastern Emperors worked with the Popes of Rome.

The answer to this is simple in one sense : they worked together about as badly as possible, and as they had constant opportunities of quarrelling, their misunderstandings grew worse and worse. But if you were to ask the reason of the bad feeling at any one moment, you would not have clear and sufficient answers given. At one time, a Roman would tell you that all people at Constantinople and those who obeyed the Emperor were sadly wrong in their religious views. At another, he might say that the Exarch at Ravenna had insulted the Bishop of Rome, and accused him to the Emperor ; at another, that the Popes were in favour of peace with some Lombard chief who ought to be regarded as an enemy. No one cause by itself would account for the gradual cleavage between East and West. The people in the two regions generally spoke different languages : Greek gradually became the official language of Constantinople, Latin remained that of Rome and of the Western Church. There was no close bond of union, and there was a great deal of jealousy, especially between the Pope of Rome and the Patriarch of Constantinople. And the dislike felt by the Romans towards any scheme or fancy which would have made Rome *not* the Middle of the World, but the subject city of a distant Emperor, grew all the stronger for her having known what good government and a lofty position meant, under the rule of one of the greatest of all her Popes, Gregory the Great.

Every reader of English history knows something of the missionary labours and of the extension of the Church in the West accomplished by this Gregory, for it was he who said of the slave-children in the Roman market, "Not Angles but angels," and who afterwards sent Augustine to Kent. But besides his work in spreading Christianity abroad, and keeping an eye on what was going on in various parts of the world, Gregory did much to set things in order at home. He occupied himself with the order of service, with Church music (we may think of him in connection with Gregorian chants), and with similar matters. But there was business of a worldly kind also, always pressing upon him. By this time the estates of the Church of Rome—the patrimony of St. Peter, as they were called—had, by gifts and bequests of pious people, so much increased, that the Popes found themselves owners, or administrators, of far-stretching domains, and a Pope like Gregory I. looked into every detail of their management. Then, again, he felt himself bound to know and provide for the wants of the poor who dwelt in Rome. And beyond all this, he kept a statesman's eye on all the political changes going on around him, and exerted all his powers to bring about a peace between the Emperor, the Lombard Kings, and the Lombard Dukes. He was not entirely

successful, but at least he made the position of the
Popes more powerful and dignified than it had ever
been before, and though that position was not kept
by some of the weaker Popes who came after him,
yet the example which he had set was not lost.

But we have not time just now to loiter among
the interesting people we meet by the way. We
must hasten to see what I have called the great
opportunity taken, though what we have seen is
quite necessary to make the event clear to us. We
have seen that there was something like a three-
cornered game going on in Italy, between the Pope,
the Lombard King, and the Exarch who represented
the Emperor. Sometimes it came to be more like a
round game—there were so many playing each for
his own hand. Thus there were the Lombard
Dukes, who, we have seen, were often opposed to
the Kings at Pavia, and there were the people of
South Italy, in great part emigrants from Eastern
lands, speaking Greek and in most things (not in
everything) keeping by the Emperor, and beyond
the Alps was the great nation of the Franks, which
had already interfered more than once in the affairs
of Italy, and was likely to do so again.

We have already learned a few things about the
Franks : first, that after they were well settled in
Gaul they had extended their dominions in all
directions ; secondly, that from the baptism of
Clovis they were Catholic Christians, not Arian
persecutors like the Vandals and some of the Goths,

nor half-hearted converts, as the Lombards seem to have been ; and thirdly, that they had *sometimes* been allied with the Goths, though the Goths found them very slippery allies in time of need.   Now it was said that before King Clovis was born, his mother had a strange vision.   First she beheld lions, unicorns, leopards, and other noble beasts moving about in the palace.   Then there were bears and wolves, devouring one another ; then these gave way to little dogs and contemptible beasts biting and snarling.   This was a parable of the first race of Frankish kings.   Clovis, of course, had been among the lions.   His sons and grandsons, among whom the kingdom was divided, were as the bears and wolves.   Before the middle of the eighth century we come to the weak, snarling dogs and cats. Finally the kings came to be called by the name they deserved, the *Do-nothings*, and the Frankish power would have vanished away but for the energy of a kind of prime minister, who held office under the King and was called " Mayor of the Palace." This minister belonged at first to only one of the kingdoms, but in course of time the office became hereditary in one family, and he who held it ruled over all Frankish countries.   One of the most famous of this family was Charles Martel (the Hammer).   While he was in power, the Mahometan Saracens pressed northwards from Spain as far as Poitiers, but the blow they received from the Hammer saved Europe from a terrible invasion.   It was to this Charles that Pope Gregory III. (not the Great) looked for help against the Lombards.

The great quarrel which led to a breaking up of the already unsettled state of things in Italy had to do with religion. After several Emperors who did not show much energy, there came a new dynasty, from Isauria in Asia Minor, which was strong enough to keep the Saracens at bay, and intelligent enough to wish to have the popular religion purified from superstitions. We have already seen how the Mahometans reviled the Christians as worshippers of many gods, even of gods made by the hands of men. The question as to the use and the abuse of objects of sacred art is an old one and not likely to come to an end so long as man is capable both of worshipping and of representing in some fashion what he worships. But the sacred symbols against which the cry of idolatry is raised are not generally beautiful works of art, but old and quaint objects which are supposed to have been brought by the hands of angels, or to which stories of miraculous powers are attached. However this may be, any Emperor or other person in authority who rides full tilt against the religious and superstitious feelings of the common people is likely to fail himself and to hand down a bad name to posterity. So was it with the Emperor Leo the Iconoclast and his son, Constantine V. In Italy, with which alone we are now concerned, both Pope and Lombards refused to accept the Emperor's orders for the removal of images. The people of Ravenna were partly inclined to the Pope's side, as they felt burdened by the imperial taxation. One Exarch was killed; his successor was driven out of Ravenna. Then, strange to say, the Pope helped to bring about the restoration of the Exarch by the Venetians. Afterwards the Pope, having taken up the cause of the rebellious Dukes, had another quarrel with the Lombard King, and the Exarch and the King marched against Rome, so that the Pope had a narrow escape. These changes in parties and sides seem strange, but we must remember again that it was a three-cornered game. The Pope looked in hope for the Hammer to appear from over the Alps, but the Hammer was otherwise engaged.

After this, for a time, the Pope was hardly pressed by Liutprand, one of the ablest of the Lombard kings. There were more shiftings and changes afterwards, but in 750 we find that the Lombard King had taken Ravenna, and the Pope, in his perilous position, could get no help from the Emperor. Accordingly Pope Stephen crossed the Alps, met Pippin, son of the Hammer and Mayor of the Palace, and promised that he would declare him to be King in name (as he was in reality), and Roman Patrician likewise, if he would come to the rescue. We cannot stop to look into the question of the right claimed by the Pope to create Kings and Patricians. Observe, however, that he did exercise that right. Pippin came, obtained possession of the lands formerly held by the Exarch, now subject to the Lombards, and put it under the power of the Pope. From this time forward, the Popes, whatever else they may be, are princes ruling over a large part of central Italy. Soon afterwards, when the Lombards had risen against the Pope and were besieging him in Rome, Pippin came once more to his aid, and forced the Lombards to submit.

Peace was kept for a time, though when Desiderius was made King of the Lombards, we find that he actually tried to make friends with the Emperor against the Pope. In 771, the last war between Popes and Lombards broke out. Desiderius had attacked Pope Hadrian I. Charles, son of Pippin (called the Great, or Charlemagne for Carolus Magnus), marched into Italy, captured Pavia, made Desiderius his prisoner, and took to himself the crown and kingdom of the Lombards.

Now, then, there is no more Exarchate, and the King of the Franks is the King of the Lombards, and doughty champion of the Pope. What need for more changes and fightings ? For one thing, the Lombard Dukes had to be made submissive. When this was done the King became Lord over all Italy, except the part in the middle which belonged to the Pope, and some parts in the South which still looked to the Emperor. He had, in 800, to use his powers to put down a tumult against a newly elected Pope, Leo III., who had been driven out of Rome by a faction. And on Christmas Day of that year the great event took place. Charles was worshipping in the Church of St. Peter, when the Pope came forward, crowned him with a golden crown, and anointed him with oil, while all the Frankish soldiers and the people round about shouted aloud : "To Charles Augustus, crowned by God, to the great peace-making Emperor, be long life and victory."

Thus the Empire was restored to Rome. Perhaps not many people knew beforehand what was going to happen. Charles afterwards said that if *he* had known, he would never have gone to church that day. Still less would any one know what the result would be. Rome had an Emperor again. Charles sat, or seemed to sit, in the seat of Augustus. But he had not, as Augustus had had, the means in his hand for administering the government of the whole civilised world. The dominions over which he ruled as *King* (to say nothing of the Empire) were vast, and increasing in vastness, as it was his task to subdue the heathen nations of North Germany, and to beat back the Saracens in Spain. He loved law and order as Trajan had done, and Theodoric, and other great rulers of men. He could issue edicts, and hold assemblies, and send round officials, and do all that a mighty king may do to keep his realm united, but could he, or his successors after him, really justify the title "great and peace-making Emperor"?

Then how about the other Empire, that ruled

from Constantinople ? Was not that properly the continuation of the Empire of Augustus and of Constantine ? How could one leave it out of consideration and crown an Emperor of the Romans as head of the whole world ? The fact is, the Empire ruled from Constantinople had become of little account to the peoples of the West. It had, as we have seen, been incapable of helping the Popes against the Lombards. It had once been heretical, and though that reproach might have died out, it was looked on as of less dignity and authority in Church matters than was the seat of St. Peter. Then—chief of all—just at this time there was no Emperor ruling at Constantinople at all, but a wicked Greek woman, who had caused her son, the Emperor, to be put down and blinded. Of course this state of things did not last. There were Emperors of the East, as we sometimes call them, or Byzantine Emperors, right down to the middle of the fifteenth century. And in course of time they acknowledged Charles and his successor and were acknowledged by them, though each would have asserted that the Empire ought to be one and indivisible.

It is difficult to enter into the minds of men of such far distant periods, but if we try to do so, we find two ideas firmly held : that Christendom needed one temporal head, as she had one spiritual head, to bind Christian men together, and to lead them against their common enemy, the Mahometans ; and that this power had been given by God, through the action of the Pope, to the King of the Franks, who had thus been made the head of the Holy Roman Empire. And though we shall see how, in course of time, it became impossible to realise this idea in practice, yet it remained all through the Middle Ages as something to be longed after and striven for :—the universal reign of a righteous sovereign who derived his power from God, and who used it, from the ancient seat of Roman authority, to curb the passions and to enlighten the minds of Christian men, and to bind the warring nations in one great brotherhood.

CHAPTER X

EMPERORS AND POPES

NOW that there is a real Emperor in Rome again, you will say, history will become more interesting and less confusing. The great procession will have come into line, and we shall be able to trace it more easily as we see crowned heads towering, at intervals in the march, over the lesser people. But alas ! the Holy Roman Empire, as the Empire of Charles, which began on Christmas Day 800, is usually called, was not, even from the first, a rule of peace and order, and though Charles and his successors were thought of as the successors of Augustus, they stood in a very different position from his. Augustus had been real governor over all the lands that looked to Rome as their head, and that meant *all* civilised lands, except some far-away kingdoms in the East, and many barbarous lands that honoured the civilisation of Rome. He was considered, we have seen, as ruling over some provinces by his imperial authority, and as sharing in the authority over

others, but really he held the reins of the government which kept the vast regions of the Empire
in some kind of order, and in obedience to the
Great City.   Charles was called Emperor; but
merely *as* Emperor, neither he nor any of his successors could have done much.   Charles was King
of the Franks, and he had also obtained the Lombard kingdom in Italy.   He had conquered the
Saxons, and driven back the Saracens from part
of Spain.   After his death, his dominions were
divided among his sons, but the Empire could not
be divided, and went to one of them only.   This,
you see, was a very different arrangement from the
divisions of the Old Empire (as among the sons of
Constantine), by which two or three might hold the
imperial title at once, and rule as colleagues over the
lands assigned to each.   The different European
kingdoms came to be quite independent one of
another.   The title of Emperor generally went with
the German kingdom, so that some people got the
notion that it meant Emperor of Germany—whereas
there never was an Emperor of Germany till a little
more than a quarter of a century ago.   The separation became more marked as Charles's dynasty died
out, and kings of other families came to rule over
the West Franks, or Frenchmen, and over the
Germans, and over some of the Italians.   The
German King generally looked on the Empire as
his right, but till he had really been crowned in
Rome it was not correct for him to take the title.

And besides claiming the title of Emperor, he always wished to keep a hold on North Italy. Now this hankering after Italy, after a coronation in the Middle of the World and the enjoyments of beholding, and calling his own, the fair lands of the South, led many a German monarch to neglect his own kingdom and to waste splendid armies in venturesome expeditions which seldom brought much good. For the Italians never loved the Germans, and the Germans could not bear the Italian climate. Rome was not the natural home of those German kings. And even if they held Rome, that did not mean much more power over the kings and kingdoms of Europe. The German Emperors were like the dog in Æsop's fable. They dropped the piece of real meat from their teeth, and never picked up the bright reflected piece in the water.

The territories over which Charles and his successors ruled were not so extensive, towards the East, as those of Augustus had been. Yet the duties of the German Emperors were not entirely unlike those of the older Emperors, in that they had to keep at bay many fierce Eastern peoples that were always threatening the countries on the Mediterranean. It was the Eastern Empire, ruled from Constantinople, that had first to make itself into a barrier against the Mahometan hosts from Asia. But the countries which owned the German Emperor as their paramount chief, and the Pope of Rome as their spiritual head, were often sorely distressed by the invasions of the Saracens, whom we have already seen as opponents of the Franks in Spain and Gaul. Part of South Italy was seized by them, in spite of all the efforts of Pope and people, the Emperor being too far away to help.

The territories, then, and also the powers of the earlier and later Emperors were very different. If we find, in the centuries after Charles, an Emperor who is of much account in Europe generally, we may be sure that he has become strong by making the most of his powers as *King*, or even as lord over his own lands. For we are coming to the times when all the great rulers were also great land-owners ; when those who had land could muster soldiers, and have their word obeyed, and obtain wealth from the men under them ; and those who had little or no land could do nothing and keep nobody in order, however magnificent their titles might sound. That is to say, we are coming to the days of Feudalism. The Emperors were at the same time feudal kings, with very independent vassals under them, and besides being kings they were often dukes, or held great estates under other titles. The great vassal dukes in Germany sometimes waged war against one another or against the Emperor, and made it less easy for him to feel himself to be the Augustus, the universal maintainer of order and peace.

But there was another, more important difference still between the old and the Holy Roman Empire. In the days of Augustus, and those who came after him, there was no division made or even imagined between spiritual and temporal authority—between the powers resting in the heads of the Church and of the State. Augustus was Pontifex Maximus, the head of the Roman religion. In so far as there was *one* religion prevailing throughout the Empire, its unity helped to strengthen the Emperor, for all but a few outsiders (whom all those about the Emperor looked on as a small crazy crew) worshipped Augustus or his genius. The Emperors whom we have to do with now might seem to have as much as the older ones had of the strength which comes from the religious reverence of the people. For the Emperor was the champion of Christendom against the infidel. He held his authority from God, and had been crowned and anointed by the successor of St. Peter. But—and here lay all the difference—he was not head of the Church as the Pope was; the Church was more to be honoured and obeyed than any human governor, and the head of the Church, the Vicar of Christ on earth, was there in Rome, in the person of the Pope. When Leo anointed Charles, he bowed before him, as if to acknowledge that the Emperor was his superior. Yet might not his supporters and successors say that it was to the Popes only that the Emperors owed their authority? Charles and Leo understood one another, but when they had passed away, the question came to be discussed, and quarrelled about, and fought out at last in deadly conflict : Is the Emperor or the Pope the real Head of the World, ruling from the City of Rome ?

The City of Rome, different as she was in all respects from the city that Augustus had rebuilt, and that Trajan and Hadrian had beautified, after all the spoiling and devastation she had suffered at the hands of Goths and Vandals and her own citizens, was as much venerated as ever. The chief thing that helped to make her the one place that everybody who could travel would like to see just once in his life, was the eagerness with which people set about making pilgrimages. We have already seen how devout people liked to pray at the shrines of great saints. There must have been some confused notions in their minds, that although the spirits of the saints were in heaven, yet they hovered around the places where their bodies rested, and were more easily to be found there than in any other place. Now, as we have seen, it was everywhere believed that the two chief apostles, St. Peter and St. Paul, had suffered martyrdom at Rome, and it was worth travelling many a weary mile and incurring great dangers to obtain the help of such powerful champions. Probably, too, the long journeys and the dangers were rather an encouragement than a hindrance to people who loved adventure and had not many interests in life of a quiet, stay-at-home kind. Rome thus became the great meeting-place for pilgrims. Not many went further, though some made their way as far as the Holy Land, to pray in more sacred places still. Among the peoples of the North who delighted in pilgrimages, being both fervent in religion and fond of adventure, were the Normans, who had been the fiercest pirates of the seas, but had early in the tenth century settled in the North of France, and become at least as civilised as their neighbours. Our travels in our own country and our readings in English history have made them familiar to us as great church-builders and as strong rulers. About fifty years before they conquered England, the Normans obtained a strong footing in Italy, and this is important for our present purpose, as they had much to do in the struggles that went on in and about Rome. The story of their conquests is an interesting one. It begins with the consent of a few Norman pilgrims to help a Lombard prince against the Saracens. It ends with the establishment of the Norman power over Lombards and Greeks and other peoples in Italy and Sicily. They almost compelled one of the popes, who had fallen into their hands, to acknowledge the rightfulness of their conquests, provided that they acknowledged him as, in some sense, their overlord. A little later, the Norman duke was recognised by the Pope as King of the Two Sicilies, or of Naples and Sicily, but that was not till after the time I am speaking of now.

We see, then, that there was at this time nothing like an orderly and harmonious government over the whole world. Some kingdoms had arisen in Europe which were certainly not under the Emperor, and did not, as a rule, pay very much heed to the Pope. And even where the sway of the Emperor and the spiritual or even the political headship of the Pope were acknowledged, there were a multitude of lesser powers—dukes set over independent peoples, cities controlled chiefly by their bishops, lesser or greater lords who had more notion of their rights over their subjects than of the rights of higher powers over them ; so that it needed all the might of Emperors and Popes combined to make men learn how to obey and to respect law and order. And unfortunately just when the union of these two powers was most needed, the great strife broke out between them.

The strife may be explained thus : the Popes wished to maintain order and obedience in the Church, and to prevent the clergy from becoming mere servants of Emperors or Kings, while the Emperors were anxious to keep all their subjects, lay and cleric, in order and in loyal obedience to themselves. So far, each party had a good cause, but though, in the conflict, some real heroism was shown by combatants on either side, yet we cannot say that either party made the most of its cause, and acted quite generously towards its opponent.

For some years after the time of Charles the Great, neither Popes nor Emperors were very strong. The Emperors were wasting their strength in trying to do things which they could not do, and the Popes seemed to have forgotten all the duties which they ought to have done. Then some strong and right-minded Emperors endeavoured after a better state of things, deposed some unworthy Popes, and put in their place men who had a higher notion of the work they were called to do. Then some Popes desired reforms which were not acceptable to the Emperors, and thus, as often happens among us poor blundering mortals, the well-meant acts of good men brought on them or their successors such troubles as, if they had been foreseen, would have discouraged any attempt to make things better.

The places whence the idea spread that the Church ought to be purified and to be kept apart from the world, were some of the most important monasteries, notably that of Clugny in Burgundy. It would, of course, be a great mistake to suppose that all monasteries were like one another. At Clugny a stricter rule was kept than elsewhere, and those who went there did not amuse themselves in luxury, but worked, and prayed, and obeyed their superior as they were bound to do. And when other monasteries had fallen into evil plight, they used sometimes to put themselves under the Abbot of Clugny, that he might reform their rule and help them in all their affairs.

Men who are very much in earnest generally manage to get a hearing some time or other, and very often they come to hold, almost against their own will, positions of power and authority whence their word sounds forth as law. So it came to pass

when men who had been at Clugny, or who held the
Clugny ideas, were made Popes.   The first great
reforming Pope was Leo IX. (or Bruno), and with
him there worked an Italian who had lived as a
monk at Clugny, Hildebrand.

Hildebrand is the man who in this period towers
above all around him, because he was one of the
very few who see clearly, from their early days, what
they mean to do, and who keep to their purpose
all their life, without flinching from any suffering
or labour that their conduct may cause to themselves or to others very dear to them.   His father
was   only   a   Tuscan   carpenter,   but   there   was
always this excellent point in the Church of the
Middle Ages, that it gave opportunities for really
clever boys or able young men to rise from a humble
position to the very loftiest.   Hildebrand's education
began in Rome, but he was early sent over the Alps
in order, it was said, that his restless spirit might be
broken in by tedious travel and severe study.   Not
only did he study, he learned something of the
world, for Clugny was, as we have seen, a kind of
mother-abbey over others that acknowledged her
rule, and as Hildebrand gradually showed that he
was made to be a ruler of men, he would naturally
be looked on as a future bishop, or even Pope.   He
visited the imperial court while Henry III. was
reigning, a reforming Emperor who had deposed
three unworthy Popes.   And when Bruno, Bishop
of Toul, was made Pope, Hildebrand, having per-

suaded him not to receive that office from the
Emperor *only*, led him to ask for the assent of
the Clergy and People of Rome. When Leo
died, Hildebrand contrived to secure that a
man of like views should succeed him, and so
we have several Popes, acting more or less under
Hildebrand's guidance, before he became Pope
himself as Gregory VII. in 1073. It is interesting
to us, English people, to know that it was during
the time when Hildebrand was not Pope, but next-
to-Pope, that William the Norman set sail for
England, promising to bring that wicked, schismatical
country back to a closer union with Rome. And
afterwards, when Hildebrand was really made Pope,
William and his great Archbishop Lanfranc were
often in correspondence with Gregory VII., who
made very high claims on the distant Church and
kingdom of our country. William did not give way
to him in all things. Lanfranc had to go to Rome
to smooth over points of difficulty. But in general,
Gregory and William respected one another, each
knowing that the other was a strong man. But we
must look a little into the ideas of reform which
monks meditated on at Clugny and the Popes tried
to carry out from Rome.

One idea, as we have already seen, was the
enforcement of discipline and good order in all
monasteries. The vows which monks and nuns
took were to be looked at seriously. No one should
ever enter a monastery unless he or she did really

mean to give up the world and lead a religious life. On the other hand, the lands and property of monasteries and of all churches were to be held sacred, and no nobleman or king might ever lessen them or injure them in any way. Among the clergy who were not monks, of course the discipline was not so strict ; but three things seemed quite necessary : they must never have wives and families, for if they had, they would always be thinking of the greatness of their children, and would not care for the good of the Church. Then they must never pay money in consideration of any office in the Church whatsoever. This would be to incur the guilt of simony. A great many offices about the king's courts at this time were always sold, and thus Hildebrand's principles were the harder to take in and all the more important to insist on. And— most important point of all—no bishops or holders of high office in the Church should be appointed by any worldly sovereign, nor receive the symbols of authority from his hand, nor swear to be faithful as his "men." For the authority they held was not of this world, and even kings should be subject to the Vicar of Christ and to those who had been commissioned by him.

It is quite plain to us why these ideas should be welcome to all those who cared about the Church, and saw in the watchfulness of the clergy and the reverence of the laity the only hope and safeguard against oppression and lawlessness in an age of violent ignorance. And it is plain also that violent and lawless kings liked to have command over the goods of all their subjects, and that those kings who were trying to restore law and order would have liked to obtain all the help they could from the bishops, who knew at least what law and order meant. In justice to the reforming Popes, I think we may say that they were quite as stern and peremptory in denouncing acts of oppression and cruelty to the people on the part of kings and nobles as they were in complaining of wrongs done to the Church. Thus when Philip I. of France, one of the worst kings of that time, seized for his own use the goods brought by foreign merchants into France, Gregory wrote and told him that he was acting like a brigand, and that if he went on in the same way his subjects should receive orders from Rome to obey him no longer. Philip was frightened, and promised to do such things no more, and if he did not keep his word to the end, that was not the Pope's fault.

But the sovereign with whom Gregory had the sharpest and most painful conflict was Henry IV. of Germany. He was the son of the excellent Emperor Henry III., and came to the throne when only six years old. During his early days, his mother, Agnes, tried to carry on the government; but the great dukes and great bishops were struggling against one another to get the upper hand, and at length one party kidnapped the young King and carried him off in a boat. His mother departed to Rome, where she became a strong supporter of the Pope. Gregory was not at first disposed to quarrel with Henry; but though he had consented to Hildebrand's election, the young King looked on the Pope as his greatest enemy. This was not unnatural, as the Pope was constantly issuing decrees against bishops who married, or allowed their clergy to marry, and who received their offices from the King; and these bishops were, in some cases, just the men that Henry was willing to trust. In the north of Italy, especially, there was a strong feeling against Gregory's rules. The Archbishop of Milan, who had been appointed by the Emperor, without the Pope's sanction, upheld the party that opposed Hildebrand, and many of the greater bishops wished for a more independent position than he would have allowed them. For Gregory would have given them very few privileges, and would, in fact, have made them his *men*, or vassals, as the dukes and counts were vassals of the Emperor. A quarrel which Henry had with his own subjects, especially with the Saxons, made many of the Germans inclined to make the most of the strife between King and Pope, in order to serve their own ends.

Gregory had not desired a lifelong quarrel with the King, still less a long civil war. He saw a worthier object for his strivings in the far East. We have seen that the Holy Land had fallen into the hands of Mahometan Arabs. Three years after

Gregory had become Pope, Jerusalem was taken by the Seljukian Turks. These people were far more fierce and intolerant than the Arabs, and Christian pilgrims suffered great cruelty at their hands. When the story of these sufferings reached Europe, many felt deeply moved, and the more enterprising spirits and the more sagacious minds turned towards the great idea of recovering for Christendom what had been the most sacred of Christian possessions. But first, the Church ought to be made united and orderly in Italy and France and Germany; then the Church of the East, with the Empire ruled from Constantinople, must be brought into union with the West. Afterwards, the Turks could not stand, and Christendom would be saved from great anxiety and would extend her borders to what they had been and should be. Unfortunately, the first of these three steps was never accomplished by Hildebrand. But it has often been remarked that *if* he had been able to do all he tried to do, in Europe and in the East, the Crusades would have accomplished far more than they actually did.

But to return to the contest between Gregory and Henry. Gregory had declared that all sacraments administered by married priests were of no effect, and that all the clergy who had received investiture from any laymen were excommunicated—shut out of the Church. Henry continued, especially after he had obtained a victory over the Saxons, to favour the excommunicated persons, and to pay no heed to

the Pope's letters. At length he held a council of
bishops at Worms—men on whom he could rely—
and a letter full of tremendous denunciation was
sent to Rome to " Hildebrand, not a Successor of
the Apostles, but a false monk," ordering him to
come down from the Papal throne. In return,
Gregory, in an assembly at Rome, issued a decree
cutting off Henry from the Church, and loosing all
his subjects from all their duties to him, even if they
had sworn fidelity.

Meantime, the great German dukes, anxious for
more independence, rose against Henry and invited
the Pope to come to Germany to settle their disputes
against him. They declared also that if Henry were
not absolved and readmitted into the Church within
one year of his excommunication, they would cease
to regard him as their king.

Henry seemed thoroughly humiliated. But perhaps he showed more spirit and discretion now than
on some other occasions. He did not want to have
the Pope in Germany. He must somehow become
reconciled to the Church. If he made his way to
Gregory before he had left Italy, and demanded abso-
lution from him, not as judge and mediator, but as
an ordinary priest, Gregory would be bound to
absolve him on the same conditions as those offered
to other penitents, and then the nobles would have,
so to speak, the wind taken out of their sails, and
the visit of the Pope to Germany might somehow be
postponed. Accordingly, in the depth of winter,

Henry, with his wife and child and a very few attendants, hurried over the Alps. Gregory was moving northward and was staying in the Castle of Canossa, which belonged to a lady much devoted to his cause, the Countess Matilda of Tuscany. Henry submitted to the very severe rules imposed on excommunicated men, standing for parts of three days barefoot in the castle court. Then he was absolved from his excommunication, and promised to agree to the decision at which the Pope might arrive when he came to Germany. This, of course, brought no settlement. The Pope never found the way to Germany open to him. The German dukes chose another king, and a war began which lasted for twenty years.

Gregory seems to have really wished to mediate, but finally he recognised the anti-king, Rudolf, and excommunicated Henry once more. When Henry felt strong enough, he denounced Gregory as he had done before, and induced the German and Lombard bishops to choose another Pope. This was, of course, irregular and illegal; but rules count for little when war is raging. Then Henry marched on Rome. The Pope held some strong places, especially the Castle of St. Angelo, which had been the tomb of Hadrian. Henry was crowned Emperor by the anti-pope whom he had brought with him. Gregory, in sad distress, called upon the only power in Italy now able to deliver him, the Norman duke, Robert Guiscard.

Robert had not hitherto thrown himself very heartily on the Pope's side, and just now he was engaged in a war against the Eastern Emperor. He came, however, obtained entrance into Rome, forced Henry to retire, and released the Pope from present danger. Then followed a terrible time for Rome. Ancient monuments were destroyed, houses burned down, citizens sold into slavery. Then Robert marched southwards, taking Gregory with him. The Pope, now an aged man, and shaken by all that he had gone through, was carried to Salerno, and there, the next year (1085) he died in exile.

He never doubted that his was the right cause. " I have loved righteousness and hated iniquity," were the words he kept repeating as he lay dying. So, no doubt, he had done. But when one sees by what terrible means the cause which he regarded as the righteous one had been served, we cannot but wish that he had also hated all iniquitous ways of furthering righteousness among men.

CHAPTER XI

KINGS AND POPES

AFTER reading the story of Hildebrand and Henry IV., you naturally ask: Which won in the end? Not Hildebrand, who died in exile, nor yet Henry IV., who in his later days was worn out and broken-hearted by strife with undutiful sons and rebellious vassals. Then which *cause* prevailed? That, again, is a question not quite easily answered. When we try to follow the great conflicts, whether of words, or of armies, or of both, that have happened in bygone days, and have sometimes stretched on for years or even centuries, we commonly find that when an end is made, not only the persons fighting, but the objects fought for, are quite different from what they had been at the beginning. Generally each party gains or loses something that it had wanted all along, and gains or loses something that it had not cared about till the fight was half over. So it was in the struggle between Popes and Emperors. The original question about lay investitures—as to whether bishops and abbots might receive the symbols of authority from the emperor or king whose subjects they were to be—was settled by an arrangement in which each side gave way a little. Those who held spiritual authority were only to receive the signs of that authority, the ring and the crozier, from some clerical person. But they might do homage to the king and swear fealty to him in consideration of the lands they held within his dominions. This compromise was first agreed on in England, where the best of our archbishops, Anselm, had been supporting the claims of the Pope against Henry I., one of the ablest of our kings, and practically the same agreement was made between the Emperor Henry V. and the Pope Calixtus II., some twenty years later. But the root of hostility remained, and had plenty of opportunities to crop up again after the trunk had been lopped away. And the constant quarrels wearied and wore out both parties, more particularly the Empire, until the Emperors gradually came to the conclusion that they had better give all their attention to Germany, and most of it to their own hereditary dominions in Germany. Those of them that had most spirit, however, clung for a long time to the hope of getting a strong grasp on Italy and of retaining Rome as their capital city, in fact, and not only in word.

Meantime, one of Hildebrand's ideas may have seemed to be realised. At the preaching of one of

Gregory's successors, a Crusade had been undertaken, and many thousands of men—sometimes taking wives and children with them—had poured eastward, to recover the Holy Land from the Mahometans. In a manner, the First Crusade had been a success. After many labours and sufferings, Jerusalem had been taken, and a Christian nobleman had been set, first as Baron of the Holy Sepulchre, then as King, over Palestine, with princes ruling under him in Antioch and other cities. But this movement was executed in a hap-hazard way, and left few good results. Eastern and Western Christendom, instead of being bound together, were further estranged than ever. The Emperor who ruled at Constantinople hoped that the Crusade would help him to recover his lost possessions in Asia. But when the swarms of Crusaders came into his dominions, spoiling his country and treating him and his people as heretics, he and his people in return treated the invaders as barbarians, and were only too glad to get them across the sea and out of the way. The kingdom of Jerusalem was anything but an orderly one, and before long it was lost again to another Mahometan tribe, and even the arms of our King Richard I. could not win it back again. In the Fourth Crusade, at the beginning of the thirteenth century, the arms of the Christians were actually turned not against the Turks or Arabs, but against the very power that most needed Christian assistance—the Emperor at Constantinople. The reigning dynasty (the Greek, we may now call it) was expelled, and a western noble, the Count of Flanders, became Emperor. In about half a century, the Greeks recovered their own again, and for nearly two hundred years kept the Turks from pressing on into Europe. But, as we all know, they did not succeed, mainly because the zeal of the Crusaders had been turned aside into a number of petty channels, whereas *if* the grand ideas of Hildebrand had been followed up, there might never have been a Sultan at Constantinople, and our modern statesmen might have had less anxiety about the affairs of the East. Of course I do not mean to say that *nothing* came of the Crusades, but that they did not achieve the one thing which was their first object. They led to a great deal of activity on the sea, to an increase of trade, and to wealth and power in some of the coast towns, such as Marseilles, Genoa, and Venice. And they led to the formation of new orders of Knights, especially of the Knights Templars, whose great duty it was to guard the Holy Sepulchre at Jerusalem. We shall hear of this order by and by. I must go back to the dealings of the Popes with the great princes of Europe.

Let us see for a moment of what kind the relations between the Popes and such princes must be— princes, I mean, such as the French, the English, and the Spanish kings, who never claimed to be emperors, and so were never the Pope's rivals for universal dominion. Now in the first place, the

Pope, as spiritual head of the Christian world, was bound to keep them, as far as possible, at peace one with another, and they, as his dutiful sons, ought, he considered, to submit their quarrels to his arbitration. At the time when the Crusades were being preached, the Popes naturally desired that all Christian nations should cease their disputes and join together against the Mahometans. And at all times, this peace-making function was one deemed especially suitable to the successor of those who first preached the Gospel of Peace. When the Pope, in virtue of this duty of his, went on to exhort men to use force against violent and unjust rulers who would not keep the peace, many people thought that he was going too far. But that was partly because they were not sure that the Pope was considering entirely and impartially the good of his whole flock.

Then again there were sundry rights which the Pope claimed as head over the clergy in the churches of various countries. We have seen already some of his claims as to giving the symbols of authority to the bishops and abbots. He also claimed the right of actually appointing bishops and granting church livings and posts in cathedrals to the clergy, under various circumstances which I cannot go into now. This was a very vexatious right when he gave appointments to men who did not belong to the nations in which their duties lay. In early times it was a good thing, and helped to

14

bring people closer together, that a clergyman could be made at home all the world over. Thus one of our most useful archbishops of early days came from Tarsus in Cilicia, and I have already mentioned the saintly Anselm who was an Italian and had lived also in France. But as the different nations grew more distinct one from another, they preferred to have their clergy chosen from their own people and able to speak their language; and foreign bishops often preferred to stay away from their sees, and take the money without doing any work. It was also a recognised thing that the Popes should tax the clergy, and in that case the clergy must somehow get the money from the laity, and would not, even then, have much to spare for king and country. And there was a further great difficulty about the law-courts. The clergy claimed to be tried by different courts and according to different laws from those of the rest of the world, and some of the wrong-doings of laymen were considered to deserve punishment in church-courts. And if justice seemed to have been denied, the person who had a grievance might appeal beyond the King to the Pope himself, and thus the Pope seemed to be put in a certain way above the King.

But there was one difficulty worse than all the rest, or rather one which made all other grievances tenfold heavier, the Pope himself had become an Italian prince, more interested in the affairs of Italy than in those of any other part of the world. We have seen that from the time of King Pippin he had reigned over part of Central Italy ; and the Countess Matilda of Tuscany, the brave champion of Hildebrand, had bequeathed large dominions to the Pope of Rome for ever. So that when he commanded princes to be at peace, or levied taxes, or summoned offenders to Rome, he seemed to be contriving means for putting down his own enemies in Italy, rather than for advancing the welfare of the Christian Church.

In reading English history, you must have seen how great were the claims of the Pope, sometimes urged by men more eager about them than the Pope himself. You will remember such exciting events as the murder of Thomas à Becket, whose quarrel with Henry II. arose first about the clergy law-courts ; and perhaps you know, too, how Henry III. was braved by Simon de Montfort and the English barons, at the time when the king had joined with the Pope to fill all the best posts in the English Church with foreigners, and to send English money abroad to help the Pope in his Italian quarrels. The son of Henry III., our great King Edward I., was of a very different mind from his father in these matters, but being a man whose character was generally respected, he did not, in spite of his occasional rough dealings with the clergy, earn a place in history among the persecutors of the Church, as his contemporary did, Philip the Fair of France.

Before Philip's time, the Popes and the kings of

France had generally been on good terms. These kings of France had led crusading armies to the East. In fact, the French altogether took such a large share in the Crusades, that all western Europeans are still called *Franks* by the people of the East. And it was to a French prince that the Pope had looked for help in South Italy against the claims of the emperors and their children. You will remember how Naples and Sicily had become a kingdom under a Norman nobleman. This Norman royal family dwindled down to an heiress who was married to the son of a great and powerful emperor, Frederick Barbarossa (Red-beard), so that his son, another Frederick, "the Wonder of the World," inherited Naples and Sicily as well as his German lands.

The story of these two great Fredericks is well worth reading. Both of them were anxious to make their power in Italy a real thing, and both met with a stout resistance from the Popes and also from some of the chief cities of Italy. For many of those cities, which a little later became the nurseries of art and poetry and everything that is beautiful, were becoming wealthy by trade and fond of independence. Their fancy for governing themselves and becoming little republics was naturally not agreeable to the emperors, but they did not often come into Italy, and the Popes were always ready to encourage them in standing up for their liberty, because they were so useful in the conflicts with the emperors. These cities were, in the north of Italy, formed into Leagues, and when they put forth all their strength, they gave sore trouble to both the Fredericks. Most unfortunately, they were always quarrelling with one another, as did the Greek cities of old, and they never joined all together into one community. In South Italy and Sicily there were fewer great cities, but there was a strong kingdom, and the land was fertile and beautiful. The great Emperor Frederick II., whose story I cannot stop to tell you now, settled some Saracens in his Neapolitan kingdom—which seemed a wicked thing to many people at that time. His son and grandson after him claimed the kingdom and were resisted by the Pope, who declared that he was the chief ruler of it, as the Normans had themselves acknowledged. At last the Pope called in a French prince, Charles, a brother of the great crusading king, Louis IX. He conquered most of the country, and remained on intimate terms with the Pope. But his rule was harsh and stern, and it soon appeared that Italians, especially Sicilians, and Frenchmen do not easily get on together. Meantime, the king and princes of Aragon (Spain was not as yet all one kingdom) put in a claim, because a lady of the Hohenstauffen family (that to which the Fredericks had belonged) had been married to one of their kings. The war between French and Spaniards for South Italy went on for a long time. In the end, the children of the French prince to

whom the Pope had offered the crown (not the
kings of France, but a younger branch of the royal
family) kept the kingdom of Naples, and a younger
branch of the Aragonese family kept Sicily. But
this was not settled till after a long time.

Meanwhile, Italy was in a very distracted state.
One reads of the factions of the Guelfs and Ghibelins.
These names were used in different senses at different
times, but generally the Guelfs were the party of the
Popes, the Ghibelins that of the Emperors—especially of the two great Fredericks and all their
descendants. So strong was the party spirit everywhere, in the country, and the cities, and even
among the cardinals who had to choose the Pope,
that it seemed as if there would never be any chance
of peace and unity in the Italian cities, and in the
Roman Church, and in Christendom generally. In
1292, a new Pope ought to have been chosen in
place of one who had just died. But among those
who had to choose, some were Italian and others
French, and of the Romans some favoured one
great family and others an equally great family at
daggers-drawn with the other ; so that for a whole
year there was no Pope at all, and nobody saw
where one was to come from. Then at last a
strange thing happened. The men who had been
trying to outwit one another and each to make their
own party prevail, were suddenly moved to choose
a Pope who belonged to no party, and whose only
recommendation was that he was supposed to be a

very holy man. Some of the cardinals began to speak of the wonderful virtues of a poor man who lived by himself in the mountains, named Peter Morrone. An archbishop, two bishops, and two notaries were sent to search for him that he might be made Pope. They found him in his cave, clothed in haircloth, and living on bread and water. With great difficulty they persuaded him to come down. Two kings held his bridle as he rode on an ass into the city of Aquila (he could not be brought any nearer to Rome), and he was made Pope, taking the name of Celestine V. As might have been expected, his rule was an utter failure. He knew nothing of the world, and soon fell into the hands of designing persons. He was always being asked for gifts, and of course he was always ready to make promises. Then he forgot what he had promised to one man and granted it to somebody else. He made new cardinals, almost all of one party, so that the others became very angry. When Advent came, he longed to return to his old life of prayer and fasting. At last he abdicated and fled away. His enemies pursued him, fearing lest he might be set up as Pope once more. Very soon after he died in prison. He was afterwards honoured as a saint, yet some men looked on him as a coward who had lost a splendid opportunity of reforming the Church.

His successor was a man of very different stamp, an Italian, Benedetto Gaëtani, who took the name of Boniface VIII., and was enthroned in Rome in great splendour. He was a man who attempted such great things, and who made himself so much hated by those who afterwards told his story, that it is not quite easy for us to make up our minds what manner of man he was. But one thing is very clear : he was determined to make the Papacy the great ruling power in Europe, to which all kings were to be subject.

Let us notice here that we are coming to a conflict rather different from that between Popes and Emperors. In the earlier quarrel, there was no doubt that Rome was the Middle of the World, and that whichever power—the Papal or the Imperial —had the upper hand in it was the head of Christendom. Now we find the different kingdoms of Europe refusing to allow the existence of any one dominant power ruling from Old Rome. The Pope was, of course, held in honour, and regarded as the successor of St. Peter. Yet in their wars and treaties with one another and their dealings with their own subjects, the kings regarded the Popes as having no right to interfere. And then, as to the churches of the different countries, they too were national, and were able to manage their own affairs, under their own primates and other spiritual authorities, without yielding much more than a polite recognition to the headship of the Roman See.

And just now, as we have seen, there were two particularly able kings ruling in England and France

respectively. As *men*, Philip and Edward were
very different. But as kings, they were both working on very much the same lines. Each of them
did a great deal to organise the law-courts of his
country and to ensure that justice should be done
and order kept. Each preferred to take advice of
men of law and not to trust to powerful barons.
And each saw how much strengthened the king
would be, and how much more easily he might
obtain the supplies of money he required, if he
summoned representatives of the *people*, especially
of the great towns, to the great assemblies, at which
hitherto, as a rule, only noblemen and great churchmen had had their place. These assemblies of the
three estates, as they are called—clergy, nobles, and
commons—become a regular institution in England
and in France from the time of these two kings,
both determined, if ever kings were, to have as much
of their own way as possible.

Such men were not likely to submit quietly to the
dictation of an Italian priest—for as such they
regarded Boniface. On more than one occasion
the kings were at war. Edward was Duke of
Aquitaine as well as King of England. His sailors
were constantly quarrelling with the French sailors.
Then again, Philip was, rather later on, guilty of a
most mean act, in taking prisoner the Count of
Flanders, his vassal and Edward's ally, who was
bringing his daughter to Edward's court, to be
married to his son and heir. The poor lady died in

prison, of grief, it was said, because she was not
allowed to marry Edward II.   (We should, perhaps,
call her death a happy deliverance.)   Now in these
disputes the Pope offered his arbitration.   It was a
good suggestion, but the great mistake which spoiled
all that Boniface did was that he could not, like
Augustus, be content with *having* power, he must
needs show it in the most conspicuous way possible.
Thus he annoyed the kings by ordering them to
make peace and scolding them as if they were
naughty schoolboys.   On the second occasion, they
agreed to ask him to arbitrate, but he was to do so
as Benedetto Gaëtani, not as Boniface; as himself,
that is, not as Pope.   And when he had made some
arrangement between them, they complained that
it was not a fair one; but probably such complaints
are not uncommon, even against the most just of
peacemakers.

But the great cause of dispute between the Pope
and Philip the Fair was on the subject of taxation.
Both Philip and Edward had required the clergy
of their kingdoms to contribute in at least as large
a proportion as their lay subjects in the taxation of
the realm.   In 1296 appeared a bull of Pope Boniface declaring that the clergy were never to pay
taxes, levied on Church property, to any layman
without the express consent of the Pope.   Princes
who raised such taxes were excommunicated.   Both
kings replied by pretty prompt action.   Edward,
who had a legal mind, declared that those who did

not contribute to the expenses of the government
had no right to its protection. The clergy, therefore, were to be held as outlaws. In the end, he
obtained what he wanted from them by separate
bargains, and the storm blew over. In France,
Philip issued orders prohibiting the exportation of
any gold or silver. If the clergy would not make
any payments to the King, they certainly should not
to the Pope. Boniface was not disposed to make
the King into a permanent enemy. He partly
explained away the severest sentences in the bull,
but continued to remind the King of his duties to
the Church. Philip set his lawyers to work to
frame a very fair-sounding answer, in which among
other reasonable remarks was an objection to using
the word *Church* so as not to take in laymen.
They asked whether Christ had died for the clergy
alone, and quoted the text—often appealed to in
these quarrels—" Render to Cæsar the things that
are Cæsar's." For a time, Boniface practically gave
way. But the best of arguments and of quotations
do not always settle matters about which men's
feelings have been violently roused. In 1300, Boniface seemed to be in the grandest position possible.
He had proclaimed a jubilee year, and promised
great privileges to all pilgrims who should, before
it was over, come to worship at the tombs of the
apostles. When he saw the vast concourse of
people who, in answer to his invitation, thronged
the streets of Rome, he is said to have declared, as

he stood in his purple robes, that he was the successor not only of the Popes but of the Emperors. Three years more, and he had come to an ignominious end.

The bad feeling between the two parties in this great quarrel had not really died out, and soon revived actively. For one thing, the Pope had acted very harshly towards one of the great families in Rome, and some members of that family had gone to Philip's court, and were longing for revenge. In almost every Italian city at that time there were two or three great families on the worst possible terms with one another, and their servants bore arms and were continually meeting and fighting in the public squares. In fact, the groundwork of the story of "Romeo and Juliet" is no fancy of Shakespeare's, but represents the general state of affairs. In Rome, the two great families were the Colonnas and the Orsini, and as Boniface had favoured the Orsini and punished the violent acts of the Colonnas by taking away their honours and goods, he had exposed himself to the bitter hatred of a great and powerful house. Then again, the Pope had sent as legate, or ambassador, into France, a man who had as little tact or discretion as he had himself, and Philip actually had the legate seized and imprisoned, although he was a bishop. When the Pope again wrote and reminded him that after all he was a subject of the head of the Church, Philip called, as I have already mentioned, an assembly of the Three

Estates of the Realm, and letters were drawn up to Pope and cardinals, the French clergy—whether from fear or from conscience—upholding the King's cause. Boniface summoned the principal French bishops to a council in Rome. Philip forbade them to leave the country. When Boniface had at last clearly declared that it was quite necessary for every Christian to believe that every human being is subject to the Pope, there seemed no more chance of reconciliation. At last Boniface sent a legate to Paris with a list of charges against the King, many of which, relating to his injustice and rapacity, were doubtless well founded. Philip's answers being unsatisfactory, he was to be excommunicated unless he submitted within three months.

But Philip was backed up by all his people, and had no fear of the Pope's threats. His lawyers now drew up a list of charges against the Pope, far more unreasonable than those against Philip. Boniface was called a heretic : he had said that Frenchmen had no souls, or at least he had said that he would rather be a dog than a Frenchman, and that implied that he did not believe in the immortality of the soul. But the attack was not one of words only. In the heat of the summer of 1303, William of Nogaret, one of the cleverest of Philip's lawyers, and one of the injured Colonnas made their way into Italy, and came upon Boniface in his native place of Anagni, to which he had gone for a season of rest. He was an old man now, and the people around him were not zealous in his cause. In the bitterness of his soul, he gave himself up to the ruffians who had seized him, while his house was pillaged, contrary to the orders of Nogaret, if Nogaret spoke the truth afterwards. But the people of Anagni soon felt pity and sorrow for the great man who had fallen so low. They brought him gifts of food, then insisted on his liberation, and some Roman friends with a band of soldiers came and carried him back to Rome. But his sufferings, though he was ready to rejoice in them, had broken his strength. In the October of that year he died.

Boniface had not made the most of his cause, as Hildebrand had done. He had been too noisy, had insisted on his rights in extravagant language, which he sometimes had been obliged to explain away, and had mixed himself in the quarrels of warring nations and rival families. Yet he *had* a cause for which much might have been said, and *if* the Papacy had made good its claim to keep all European nations in peace and unity, it would have satisfied a need felt by all civilised powers to this day.

The successor of Boniface was inclined to follow the same lines, and began by excommunicating the murderers, but his reign lasted less than a year. Then the King of France used all his influence with the cardinals and secured the election of a Pope after his own heart, one who did all that Philip wished so readily that a story came to be told—it is now known to be false—that there had been a secret meeting and a bargain between them. The murderers of Boniface (Nogaret and his friends seemed really to deserve that name) were reconciled to the Church ; several French cardinals were created, and Philip was allowed to have plenty of money from funds belonging to the clergy. There was one thing, however, which Pope Clement V. made some difficulty in doing, though he did it in the end. This was the suppression of the Order of the Knights Templars.

The way in which this was done forms one of the most disgraceful stories of a bad time. The only reason for attacking this great order was that it was wealthy, and the European sovereigns, especially Philip, coveted its wealth. Many of the chief knights were invited, hospitably, they thought, into France, suddenly arrested, and then tortured till they confessed all manner of impossible crimes. Many of the noblest were put to death, and a large part of their property was seized by the king.

The most notable fact about Clement V. is that he changed, for a time, the place of abode of the Popes. He took up his residence at Avignon, which belonged at that time to the kingdom of Naples, but in which he could rest under the protection of the French king. For nearly seventy years—a time generally called that of the " Babylonish Captivity " —there was no Pope in Rome, and Rome seemed to have ceased to be the Middle of the World. Yet it was just at such a time—with the war between England and France, and much fighting and rivalry everywhere—that some centre of authority seemed needed. After all, men had been so much accustomed to look to Rome that they could not help doing so still. And then they learned, or recollected, that there had been Emperors in Rome before there were Popes, and a Republic before there had been Emperors. The curious result of this thought, or discovery, we shall see in our next chapter.

CHAPTER XII

RIENZI THE TRIBUNE

ROME, then, had been left without Emperor or Pope. There *were* Emperors, of course, but they generally felt it better to keep at a distance, and if ever they came to Rome, they always spent more money than they could afford, lost many men, stirred up bad feeling between Germans and Italians, and generally did more harm than good. And there were Popes, but for about seventy years from the time when Clement V. had left Italy and taken up his abode in the city of Avignon, Rome had been deprived of her bishop and her governor, and that meant more to her than it would have meant to any other city, because she had long been accustomed to look always to the Pope and to be ruled by him. His rule might not always have been very good, but it was better than no rule at all. And the fact that she was the seat and home of the Pope had prevented Rome from ever learning how to rule herself in an orderly way, and to become strong and inde-

15   209

pendent. In the other cities of Italy, as we have already seen, it was different. Many of them, being at least *sometimes* free from the interference of powerful princes, had long been accustomed to choose their own magistrates, to defend themselves in time of danger, to settle about their trade and to keep order in their streets. But Rome had *as a town* given up her liberty into the hands of the Pope. We think so much of Rome as the Middle of the World, and of the Popes and Emperors of Rome as concerned with great affairs, that we sometimes forget that there *was* a town which needed good rules and fair courts of justice, and honest men to manage the buying and selling and other things of daily life just as much as they are needed by any other town. At one time, the Senate (which kept its name, though it was *very* unlike the old Senate) used to manage town affairs, and to be elected by the people. But I am not sure whether the elections were ever quite free, and in course of time the number of senators became very small, sometimes there were only two, or there might be only one, and they or he had to swear obedience to the Pope. True, there were other councils, and it was considered that *all* the people might meet together and say whether they approved or not of what was being done. But, practically, the People of Rome were not nearly as powerful as the People of Florence, or Milan, or the other great cities of Italy.

The reason of this chiefly was that in other cities,

the people who traded or who worked with their brains or their hands had early banded themselves together into companies or guilds, and had insisted on their rights till those who did *no* work but claimed all the privileges had been obliged to give way. In Rome, there were trade companies, but they never became powerful, and the nobles always had more to do with affairs, either in keeping order or in preventing order from being kept, than the nobles of Tuscany or Lombardy.

But was this such a bad thing for Rome, after all ? We have come across two sorts of nobles in old Roman times, the proud Patricians, who liked to hold the power in their own hands, but used it to keep the enemies of Rome in fear, and the later nobles, patricians or plebeians, who were narrow and jealous of their privileges as a class, but who were very proud of being consuls and prætors and who cared a great deal about what they might do for Rome, even if they did it in a wrong-headed way. But the Roman nobles of the fourteenth century were of a different kind. They did not hold together as a class, but each family was always in fierce conflict with some other family—as happened, we have seen, with the Colonnas and the Orsini. They had their dwellings in Rome, and liked to be senators and great men in Rome. But they were not a city-nobility. They had their strongholds in the country round, and armed men to carry out their wishes. They fought against one another, stole the goods of merchants who passed their way, gave shelter to thieves and murderers, and made the whole country unsafe. Most of them were both ignorant and violent, and those who were able to care about books and music and civilised life were often not much better, in their *acts*, than the others.

Then there was another power that partly over-shadowed the City of Rome. This was the Kingdom of Naples, founded, you will remember, by the Normans, now held by a family of French origin, closely connected with the Papacy. The Kings of Naples were sometimes called Senators of Rome, and at all times they had great influence there, and were on intimate terms with some of the Roman nobles.

Without Emperor, or Pope, or a free people, or a patriotic nobility, without independence or any real dignity, what had Rome still left to her? She had her memories of the past, and these were strong enough to make some dreamy people shut their eyes to the miseries of the present, and to make those who were eager or ambitious set their hopes on better days to come. Christians who visited the four hundred and sixteen churches of Rome thought of it as the rightful abode of saints and martrys. Students who explored the fallen temples and theatres, and puzzled out the inscriptions scattered about on neglected slabs or stones, seemed to live again in the home of the Scipios, of Augustus, of Trajan, and longed to bring back its glories.

More than one fiery soul made some attempt to do so, but failed lamentably. Rome was like a lazy schoolboy who has clever parents, and can never live up to his name. Among those who failed there was one who seemed to come so near to brilliant success that all after ages have felt interested in his story. This was Nicolas, son of Lorenzo, or, as the Italians, who love short names, called him, Cola di Rienzo. We will keep to the name of Rienzi, by which he is generally called in history, though we must remember that this was not his surname.

Rienzi was born in Rome in or about the year 1313. His father was a small inn-keeper, his mother a washerwoman, but he received a good book-education, and after spending some years at Anagni, came to Rome and settled there when he was about twenty years old. I say *book-education* because Rienzi became very well acquainted with many of the best works of Latin literature and could enjoy histories of Old Rome (especially that of Livy) and the works of the Latin philosophers. Yet he had none of the training in self-control, practical good sense, courage, and readiness, which the ancient Romans had thought more important than anything else. For that reason, even his literary training was likely to lead him astray, since he could never really understand the life of Old Rome as some men could who had read less about the Romans but done more of the things they used to do. However this may be, he adopted the profession of a notary, but seems to have concerned himself less with business than with study and dreaming. In course of time he married and had three children. He was becoming a conspicuous man, chiefly by his powers of speech, for the Romans loved to hear eloquent orations. Thus he was chosen to go on an important embassy to Pope Clement VI. at Avignon in the year 1343.

The Roman people were not disloyal to the Pope, though they regarded him as somewhat of a deserter. But they had no respect for the men whom he set over them as senators, and at this time they had just driven away the two men who held that office, and chosen a Council of Thirteen to govern instead. The object of the embassy was to assure the Pope of the loyalty of this new government, to entreat him to come back to Rome, and to beg him to proclaim a Jubilee, with promises of spiritual good to pilgrims, for the year 1350. The Pope received the deputation with kindness, accepted the acknowledgment of his rights, promised to proclaim a Jubilee, and announced his intention of coming to Rome as soon as France and England were at peace. (The Hundred Years' War between them had not long begun!) Rienzi wrote home in delight, calling on the City to make herself worthy of the Pope's presence. Cicero, Cæsar, Metellus, Fabius (a motley crew! we might say) had received honour from the Romans, when they had triumphed by fighting and bloodshed. Of how much greater admiration was Clement worthy, who came to bring peace and joy!

In point of fact, however, Clement never came, and Rienzi did not long continue in the same joyful frame of mind, since he fell into trouble at Avignon through the enmity of the Cardinal John Colonna, one of the great family which had so much power at Rome. At length, however, Rienzi returned to Rome, on good terms with both Pope and people, and holding a small office in the Papal court. His chief work, however, was among the Roman people. He eagerly took up the cause of those poor people who found it difficult to get their demands attended to, and earned the title of "consul for widows and orphans." But he did not want merely to help one here and there. He hoped to work on the minds of the people, and to bring about a thorough change in the state of the City, such as the little revolution of 1343 had failed to bring about.

The Italians are generally fond of seeing with their own eyes representations of the thoughts that their leaders or teachers wish them to take into their minds. Rienzi understood this, and tried to bring his ideas before them by means of pictures. One day the people who went up to lounge around the buildings on the Capitol saw on a wall the picture of a sad, deserted widow, drifting out to sea, and her name, written above, was Roma. Around her, other suffering women, bearing the names of great cities of old—Babylon, Carthage, Troy, Jerusalem—were sinking in the deep. The virtues—temperance, justice, and the others—were lamenting the loss of Rome. Malicious beasts, interpreted to mean the unruly nobles of Rome, were blowing on the waves and heightening the storm. In heaven above hung two swords, and the apostles Peter and Paul were seen praying against the misfortunes of the unhappy City which even they could not avert.

Thus, by a picture-sermon, Rienzi tried to show the people how their City was in danger of perishing by reason of her sins, as other cities had perished long ago. Another time he preached them a sermon on an old inscription which he had found in a church and which he supposed, without much reason, to have been hidden away by Boniface VIII. This inscription was the statement of the authority given by the Senate of Rome to the Emperor Vespasian. If Rienzi had studied Roman history with a cool head, he would have known that by the time of Vespasian the Senate had little real power to give, and that its fine-sounding words meant very little. But at least the moral that he drew from his text was good. The old Romans had been great and powerful because they had kept the laws and lived peaceably and honestly. Their descendants might recover what they had lost if they would amend their ways, and especially make peace among themselves and prepare for the approaching Jubilee.

But deeds were wanted more than sermons, and Rienzi prepared to act by calling together some of the Romans whom he thought he could trust on the

Aventine Hill, the refuge for the poor and the slaves in ancient times. Then he set forth his idea of bringing good order into the City. Those who listened wept, and promised, in penitence and hope, to follow out the great design. This was at the beginning of Lent, in 1347. The great step was taken at Whitsuntide, for Rienzi wished to make his work evidently appear as suggested and accomplished not by his own inventions and desires but by the power of the Holy Ghost.

Accordingly on the night before Whit Sunday, he passed some hours in church, preparing for his great task. Next morning, he rode through the City with a chosen band of twenty-five men, bearing four banners, with the devices of Rome, St. Paul, St. Peter, and St. George. By the side of Rienzi rode the Pope's Vicar, the Bishop of Orvieto, now zealous in the cause. They came to the Capitol, a crowd gathered round them, and Rienzi set forth the present misery of the City and the glory in which she had once shone and which she might yet recover. The assembled people listened with delight, and eagerly assented to the new laws proposed by him.

These laws do not seem very high-flown or remarkable. Murderers were to be punished with death. Accused persons were not to wait for trial more than fourteen days, and false accusers were to be punished. From the different quarters of the City, men should be provided to serve on foot or as horse-soldiers, whenever the State required them. The taxes were to be spent for the good of the people. The nobles were not to have fortresses within the City, nor to control the bridges and gates, and there were to be heavy fines taken from all who protected criminals. A ship should be provided to keep the coasts near Rome safe for merchants.

Good laws, every one saw, would be of no use without some strong power to carry them out, or at least to *begin* the new order. The Senators were sent away, and the people declared that Rienzi should have full and independent authority. In fact, they made him what the old Greeks would have called a Tyrant. The title which he preferred to take was that of *Tribune*. His readings in Roman history had taught him how the early Tribunes in Rome, and the Gracchi afterwards, had been the champions of the poor and the oppressed. But his power was very different from theirs. His full title ran: "Nicolas, by the grace of our Lord Jesus Christ, Tribune of Liberty, Peace and Righteousness, Severe and Merciful, Illustrious Liberator of the Holy Roman Republic." He varied the expressions sometimes, so as to make himself the champion of Italy and friend of all mankind, and he added the word *Augustus* (by which, however, he did not claim any rights as *Emperor*) to that of *Tribunus*. It was not decided for how long he should hold this office. He afterwards declared that he would have desired to lay it down after three months. But the people felt that he could not be spared.

For a short time everything went excellently. Powerful evil-doers, even nobles and priests, were brought to justice. The great families first sneered at the Tribune, then thought best to agree to his plans or to quit the City, and give up the possessions they had violently seized to the rightful owners. Old family feuds were, or seemed to be, made up. Rome became at least a safe place to dwell in, and the accounts were well looked into, so that the poor might be relieved from heavy taxes. The Pope wrote to express his approval and to bid the Tribune and the Vicar continue what they had begun. Rienzi enlarged his plans to take in all Italy. Letters were sent to cities near and far, telling them how Rome had become free and asking them to join in making all Italy happy and prosperous. The messengers from Rome were generally well received ; ambassadors flocked in from all around, both from free cities and from those that had fallen under the power of a lord. Even the great Kingdom of Naples acknowledged some kind of supremacy in the Roman government. There had lately been very painful events in "the Kingdom" as it was called. The Queen, Joanna, had been accused of murdering her husband. His brother was in arms, demanding revenge. Both parties sent to the Tribune, asking him to judge between them. One of the most violent of the Italian nobles, the Præfect John

da Vico, was compelled to surrender, and to give up
the stronghold which he had filled with his own
men, and whence he had done great damage to
many places near Rome. The victory was gained
for Rienzi by some of the great men who had at first
opposed his new ideas. His friend at Avignon, the
poet Petrarch, wrote a very fine poem in his honour,
celebrating the recovery of poor, decrepit Rome at
the touch of his hand, and the driving forth of the
noxious beasts who had worked her so much harm.

If our story might stop here, we should take our
leave of Rienzi as of one of those great men who
have accomplished almost impossible tasks because
they have lost all thought of themselves, of the
difficulties they must encounter and the risks they
must run, in the feeling of a mission to be accomplished and of a Divine power working in and
through them. Unfortunately, Rienzi was not great
enough to forget his own merits or to think little
of his own success. He had an Italian's love of
grandeur and display. He had a wife, children, and
other relations whose position he wished to im-
prove. He loved fine speeches, and could not let
his actions speak for themselves, or even leave them
to the verses of Petrarch. In short, he failed, as
greater men than he have failed (Alexander among
others), to keep his judgment firm and his conduct
reasonable when he saw great men cowering before
him and heard the voice of flattery on every side.
Possibly he thought that magnificence and luxury

would raise his reputation among the Roman people, and did not consider how dangerous it would be for him to raise up any enemies or give occasion for scandal.

In the month of August, two very magnificent ceremonies were held, to which all the great cities of Italy, which he now declared to be sharers in the citizenship of Rome, were invited to send deputies. On the day which commemorated one of the great victories of Augustus, Rienzi caused himself to be solemnly dubbed Knight of the Holy Ghost, by an ancient citizen who was supposed to represent Rome. Before the ceremony, he bathed in a basin of porphyry in which, legend said, the Emperor Constantine had been cleansed from a grievous disease. Afterwards he held a high-sounding discourse, in which, among other claims, he asserted the right of himself and the Roman people to decide between rival candidates for the Empire. Much feasting followed, and the people were delighted to find wine spouting from the statue-horse of Marcus Aurelius, on the Capitol. The deputies of the various cities took off their gorgeous robes and let the common people pick them up. Fourteen days later, Rienzi was solemnly crowned in the church of Santa Maria Maggiore. The Pope's Vicar had already thrown off all connection with Rienzi in disgust, but there were illustrious bishops and laymen ready to present him with seven gifts, symbolical of the sevenfold grace of the Holy Ghost.

There were crowns of oak, ivy, myrtle, laurel, olive and silver, and a silver apple surmounted with a cross. As he received these, Rienzi declared that he had achieved his triumphs in the same year of his life (the thirty-third) in which Christ had conquered the powers of evil. In after time he agreed with his accusers that these words and the whole proceedings were almost blasphemous in character. But for a time no pretensions seemed presumptuous to him. Soon after, a deed of rash violence proved—if proof were wanting—that he could not stand on a pinnacle without becoming giddy, and falling.

This deed was the arrest of seven great Roman nobles, on mere suspicion, after he had asked them to a friendly feast. True, he set them free shortly afterwards, and even gave them fresh honours, but he had made them his enemies for life, and the curious excuse he made—that he had only done them good by causing them to confess their sins and prepare for death—was one that satisfied nobody. The Pope was exceedingly angry, for some friends and relations of these nobles were about his court. Rienzi felt obliged to give way, and to drop some of his high-sounding titles. Soon after, news came that the Colonnas were entering Rome at the head of an armed force, to take vengeance on the Tribune for the insults they had received. Rienzi showed but little tact or courage. However, his forces triumphed, and a very fine young man of the Colonna family was killed. The insolence with which Rienzi rejoiced over the bodies of the slain, and sprinkled their blood over his son, as he dubbed him Knight, degrade him in our eyes more than all the childish folly that had gone before.

But the Colonnas were only the more eager for revenge. The Pope was angry with Rienzi because he had turned his back upon his legate. The people were tired of his government, especially since he had been obliged to increase the taxes. Accordingly, when the Colonnas obtained the aid of a certain Count Pepin who brought an armed force to assist them, Rienzi made no stand, but fled to the mountains. The City went back to its old form of government, a Colonna and an Orsini being the two Senators. When the great Jubilee came, and thousands of pilgrims flocked to Rome, neither Pope nor Tribune was there to receive them.

Meantime Rienzi associated himself with a brotherhood of pious men who lived apart from the world on the Apennines. They were followers of the unfortunate Pope Celestine, the predecessor of Boniface VIII., but regarded the holy St. Francis as their real founder. The friars of the order of St. Francis had not kept his rule in simplicity and entire poverty, but these men tried to go back to his life and precepts. Rienzi seems to have come among them despondent and spiritless, believing himself to have been forsaken by God and deprived of his vocation. But some of these good brethren inspired him with fresh hope. They believed, as he believed, in the speedy coming of the reign of the Holy Ghost. They showed him passages in some of their mysterious books which seemed to apply to him and to his work. At the suggestion of one of them, he left his retreat and went to Prague, where the Emperor Charles IV. then was, and offered his services to him, promising to help him if he would come to Rome and establish his power in Italy.

Neither the Emperor nor his councillors put much faith in Rienzi. They were men of common sense, and to them his promises of the coming reign of the Holy Ghost and his denunciations of the absentee Pope seemed both foolish and blasphemous. The end of his intercourse with them was that he was accused of heresy, thrust into prison, and then sent to the court of Clement VI. at Avignon.

This charge of heresy stung Rienzi to the quick, as he had always seemed to others and probably to himself to be a notable champion of Christianity. He had one good friend at Avignon, Petrarch, who deeply lamented his fallen estate. Three great churchmen were appointed to inquire into the case. In the end, Rienzi escaped the punishment of death, partly, it was said, because Pope Clement was near his end, and partly because it had been reported that Rienzi was a poet, and poetry was held in great account at Avignon. However this may be, Rienzi lay for some time in prison at Avignon, till Clement's successor, Innocent VIII., found a new occasion to put his character and talents to the proof.

As might naturally be expected, the Popes at Avignon were constantly finding that the cities in Italy which acknowledged their sway were gradually slipping away from them, and falling into the hands of some ambitious noble or some neighbouring state. Innocent VIII. was desirous of recovering his power in Rome and in other Papal dominions, and feeling unable to go himself, he sent a very able man to represent him, a Spaniard, Cardinal Albornoz. Albornoz was clever both in military and in state affairs. In fact the Pope could hardly have made a better choice. With him Innocent determined to send Rienzi into Italy, in order that the power over men which he had used to re-establish the Roman state, and had afterwards wished to employ in aid of the Emperor, might be used in behalf of the Papacy, to which, after all, Rienzi had always professed himself loyal.

In the autumn of 1353, Albornoz, and Rienzi with him, came into Italy, and as they professed themselves friends of the people and enemies of tyrants, they were in many places received with gladness, and the Papal cause began to revive. Italy had been greatly distressed lately by a terrible visitation of the plague. Another cause of suffering lay in the manner of warfare of that day. War had lately become a skilled profession, such as peaceful citizens were not likely to excel in. Consequently the Italian cities had been largely employing companies of soldiers under able military chiefs, who cared nothing about the cause they fought for, but only desired plunder and pay. Yet they were a necessary evil, and Rienzi found it desirable to make friends with two brothers, one of whom was a soldier and the other a lawyer, while their brother, Fra Moreale, was head of the greatest company of the time. Meanwhile, Rienzi eagerly inquired how parties stood in Rome, and soon found that in the disorderly state of things prevailing there, many would be glad to see him back. Accordingly he persuaded the Legate Albornoz, and the Pope himself, to let him take the title, not of Tribune, but of Senator, and try what he could do to restore order. At first his best hopes seemed likely to be realised. The Romans received him back with joy, and with the help of his new friends he succeeded in putting down many of the factious nobles of the neighbourhood. But he soon fell back into his old ways of luxurious living for himself and arbitrary violence in his dealings with others. He forced his friends, especially the brothers of Fra Moreale, to make heavy contributions towards the war. When Moreale himself came to Rome, he was seized by the Senator's orders and speedily put to death. Moreale may have been guilty of many crimes, but it was perhaps rather his wealth than any wickedness that led Rienzi, then anxious for money to pay his troops, to have him condemned.

Rienzi's conduct in Rome was henceforth marked by harshness and indecision. He again seemed to have lost all mental balance. Meantime he made an ally who might prove useful to him. About thirty-eight years before, King Louis X. of France had died, and very soon after a child was born to him, who received the name of John, was acknowledged as King, died about a week after, and thus left the throne vacant for Louis's brother Philip. Now a story was circulated that John was still alive. Those who cared for the little King, so the story ran, fearing some evil arts on the part of Countess Matilda, mother-in-law to the next heir, had taken him away and persuaded his nurse to let her child wear the royal robes on the day when the King was to be presented to the people. The wicked Countess worked her will and the child died. But it was only the nurse's child. The little King grew up, supposing himself to be the son of a weaver in wool at Siena who was the husband of his nurse. When the story of his high birth was told him, he was in doubt whether to accept it, but Rienzi persuaded him to assert his claims. If he were *really* little King John, his right would be far better than that of the present King of France, or that of the King of England who was fighting against him. But the fall of Rienzi dashed his hopes, and prevented the former Tribune from acting as a King-maker.

The end came through a combination of nobles, who knew that the people were discontented, and that Rienzi had very few friends left. An attack was made on the house which he occupied on the

Capitol.   He fled in disguise, was overtaken, and slain by the swords of the insurgents.

Some men have liked to make a hero of Rienzi. But to do so we must either shut our eyes to many very evident facts of his life, or else give up the doctrine that murder and treachery are always hateful, and that vanity and cowardice are always contemptible.   Others have regarded him as a hypocrite and impostor.   But if we take this view, we cannot easily account for the enthusiasm he once awakened in the people, an enthusiasm which did not spend itself in shouts and words, but led, for a time at least, to the establishment of a reign of peace and order.   Rienzi was not a strong man nor a clear-sighted man.   He could descend to treachery and falsehood, and could not take good fortune calmly.   But after all, he was capable of admiring a noble past, and of labouring and inspiring others to labour, towards a glorious future.   And the more we realise that he did not in many ways stand above his fellows, the more we wonder at the power of Rome, in her sacred memories and her exalted place in history, to sway the minds of men.

CHAPTER XIII

THE MEDICI POPES

RIENZI, then, had failed to restore the Roman Republic. He was gone, and there was nobody to carry out or revive his ideas. The movement he had caused was more like the ripples on the surface of a stream than the rush of the current beneath. Yet, after all, his efforts had some effect in making men see that the state of things in Italy was quite unendurable, and the Popes were obliged to understand that if they wished to keep any kind of authority in Italy, any dignity or power in Europe, they must leave their pleasant easy-going life at Avignon and settle down in Rome again, so as to recover and to keep as much as they could in spite of insolent, quarrelsome nobles in the City, independent little lords reigning in towns that the Popes had once claimed as belonging to the "patrimony of Peter," yet more independent republics, like Florence and Venice, that were practically mistresses over many lesser cities ; and last not least,

the Kings of Naples, and those who thought they
ought to be and tried to make themselves Kings of
Naples.   But though Rome was for a short time
delighted to find that she had a Pope again, before
long she found herself, to her great regret, with only
half a Pope : that is, a Pope whose authority was
only recognised in some Christian countries, while
others acknowledged his rival.   If, as we have
imagined before, we could see the most notable
persons of this period file past us in the great time-
procession, we should find some interesting figures
to look at.   There would be a simple young Italian
woman, Catharine of Siena by name, leading back
Pope Gregory from Avignon to Rome.   She had
gone the whole way to fetch him, and felt so sure
of her mission to call him back to his duty that he
also felt sure as to that duty, and came back, though
he died soon afterwards.   Then we should see a
violent, ill-tempered man whom the Italians chose
to succeed Gregory mainly because he was an
Italian, and not likely to go back to Avignon and
fall within the power of the King of France.   Then
we should not see many notable Popes in Rome
for a long space.   There was one Pope at Rome
and another, set up in rivalry to him, at Avignon.
The Avignon Popes were naturally as much connected with France as those had been who had
dwelt there during the Babylonish Captivity, though
one at least had serious quarrels with the French
king, which we cannot take up now.   France and

England were at this time, you remember, in
deadly warfare against one another, and, as you
might expect, the English acknowledged the Pope
at Rome. In like manner, whenever there was
a quarrel between two peoples, one of them was
to be found acknowledging the Roman and the
other obeying the Avignon Pope. This division
of Christendom was called the Great Schism.
Every one, even the Popes themselves, said it
was a great scandal and very mischievous to the
Church and the world. Yet it went on for more
than thirty-five years, in spite of all the efforts of
kings and statesmen and learned doctors, till at
last an end was put to it by the Council of Con-
stance, which deposed two rival Popes, and chose
another who came at once to live in Rome.

The Popes of the Restoration were not at all in an
enviable position. They were not strong in Italy.
The great leaders of soldier bands who wandered
over the country had in some cases obtained important places for themselves, and Italy now consisted of a large number of small states with a few
bigger ones, constantly combining in groups against
other groups, and making war against each other by
hiring bands of mercenary soldiers. But if the
Popes could not keep order in Italy, much less
could they do so in the distant countries of Europe.
In course of time, the great European powers began
to interfere in the affairs of Italy. The kings of
France had some kind of claim to the crown of

Naples, and in the year 1494, King Charles VIII. tried to make it good, led a great army into the kingdom of Naples and for a time conquered it. But the Italians who had reigned in Naples were related to the kings of Aragon, so that Spanish armies soon appeared upon the scene. Then the next King of France set up a claim to the duchy of Milan, and the Duke of Milan was a friend of the Emperor Maximilian, so that he, too, began to interest himself in Italy. The republican cities and the little principalities had to manage all their affairs craftily so that they might steer between their great neighbours and not be crushed by them. And the Popes, who ought to have been able to speak with authority and bid the warring states be at peace, found themselves obliged to follow much the same lines as the other powers—to hire soldiers for the defence of their territories and put them under nephews and friends who expected high rewards for their services, to ally themselves, now with this power, now with that, according as one or another became more formidable, to sell privileges and honours and to use all the mean ways that people have to follow who feel themselves to be poor and are past feeling themselves disgraced by being shifty.

This kind of behaviour on the part of the Popes, which made them seem less like spiritual heads of Christendom than like second-rate princes who had no thought for much besides their lands and their families, led some serious and learned men to ask

themselves and each other questions which were
not easy to answer. What right had an Italian
prince to stand forth as head of the Church ? Even
in the most powerful countries of Europe, at this
time, kings ruled along with some kind of parlia-
ment or council, and were not able to follow whatever line they chose. Ought not a Council of the
whole Church, such as that which had put an end
to the Great Schism, to be summoned regularly, and
to call the Pope to account if he were wasting the
blood and treasure of Christian men on his own
schemes ? We read a great deal, during the time
after the return of the one Pope to Rome, of these
claims put forward for a Council, but the Popes
managed to hold their own, chiefly because the
different nations of Europe were not sufficiently
united to insist on their rights as members of the
Church, though in some countries, especially in
England, many laws were made to keep the Popes
from having much power over bishops, clergy, and
people.

But the disunion of Christendom, while in one
way it allowed the Popes to regain strength, in
another way reduced the power and dignity which
might have made them most useful to all Europe at
that time and for many years after. This was the
period of the great conquests of the Ottoman Turks
in the East of Europe. They subdued many islands
and countries which had in old times been Greek,
and in course of time they possessed all Greece

itself and many places on the Mediterranean which
had been settled by the Venetians. Of course the
Emperors who still ruled at Constantinople ought
to have been backed up by all Europe in the attempts to keep these fierce Mahometans from
destroying all that was left of the great Christian
Empire of the East. But though in Hungary and
elsewhere a few men made a bold stand, the rulers
of Western Europe cared very little about the matter.
They looked on the Eastern Emperors as heretics and
not much better than the Turks, though some of the
Emperors were most anxious to bury all the old differences. Some of the best of the Popes of this time
were very eager to prevent the Turks from getting
Constantinople, and after they had got it, from
extending their conquests further. But they had
to give up any hope of a great crusade, though
there was talk of a crusade for many years after.
Meanwhile, in 1453, the Sultan, Mahomet II., had
laid siege to Constantinople and taken it by storm.
The last Emperor, Constantine Palæologus, was
killed, fighting bravely. Then began the rule of the
Turkish Sultans in the great city of the Eastern
Emperors, and the difficulties between Turks and
Christians in South-East Europe which have not
yet been overcome.

But if the Popes could do nothing to protect
Eastern Europe from the Turks and could not
make themselves respected in the West, and if
Rome had lost her pride and independence and

only seemed important *now*, apart from old memories, as the seat of the Pope, have we not come to
the end of the time when Rome can possibly be
regarded as in any sense the Middle of the World ?
Hardly so, as yet. There were at least some Popes
who tried to give her a headship of another kind.
They wished her to be, not only the holiest, but the
most civilised city of Europe. They wished their
court to be the most magnificent, the buildings they
raised were to be the most splendid. To Rome once
more as in old days, learned men and those skilled
in the arts were to flock, that they might find in the
Holy Father a yet more bountiful patron than
Augustus had been to the great men of his day.
Meantime, by skill in making wars and treaties, the
Popes had made themselves of great weight in Italy,
and the more magnificent they were, and the more
cleverly they chose the legates who represented
them in foreign courts and the cardinals who
belonged to various nations, the more likely would
they be to influence the kings of all countries for the
good of the Church, or at least for the good of the
papal power.

Now I want you to look a little more closely
at the most magnificent of the Popes who made
Rome great and famous by his magnificence. He
is a handsome but heavy-looking man, who generally appears smiling and pleasant, but does not seem
as if he could be stirred up himself or stir up others
to do very great deeds. The name by which he is

known in history is Leo X., though his Christian name and surname are Giovanni (or John) dei Medici. We should all feel more attracted by the fiery old Pope who goes just before him, Julius II. He is one whom everybody that goes to picture-galleries knows from a splendid portrait. He was painted by one of the greatest of artists, Raphael, who did justice to his firm countenance and noble bearing. Julius did much to make the Popes strong in Italy, especially by inducing the Italians to unite against the French, and he cared for great artists, especially for the greatest of all, Michael Angelo. Yet Leo X. is the man that gave his name to the whole period, as the great and successful Pope who nevertheless lost half Europe for the Roman Church.

Giovanni dei Medici came of a clever and successful family, the Medici of Florence. Florence, as you know, had remained a republic while many other Italian cities became subject to lords or dukes. But in Florence, as in other cities, there were several great families always living at deadly feud. At last one family rose from being ordinary citizens to obtain very great power in the state. The people of Florence were willing that they should have that power, and they generally had the good sense not to use it in a way to provoke people ; yet those who had eyes to see and minds to think perceived that Florence could not be, as she had been, a free republic, while this great family was within her walls, controlling the appointment of all magistrates, keeping up a little court, and deciding what line Florence should take in all matters of Italian politics. The Medici were banished more than once, and there had been many attempts to get rid of them before Giovanni was born, in the year 1475. But at that time his father, Lorenzo, was all-powerful in Florence.

This Lorenzo was not only a clever statesman. He was a lover of poetry and art and learning, and was one of those who helped to make the Italians the most civilised people in Europe. During his life, the movement was going on which we call the revival of letters and art, or more shortly the Renaissance. The art of painting had been practised in Italy for some centuries, and the city of Florence had many beautiful buildings which date from earlier times. But what was happening now was not only the creation of new and beautiful things, but a waking up to know how much there had been that was admirable and skilful and worthy to be remembered and copied in the works of the old Greeks and Romans, so many of which had perished at the hands of fierce barbarians or stupid and careless people who did not know the worth of what they destroyed. Among the great things which had perished were hundreds of great books which had been burned with the libraries in which they had been kept, or hidden away in monasteries. Sometimes people who could not understand the old

books, and who wanted parchment for writing fresh
stories or sermons of their own time, would endeavour to blot out the old letters and write the new
matter over them, without any thought that men of
later times would be trying with all their might to
get rid of what *they* called the rubbish on the surface,
so as to reach the *real* book hidden underneath. Of
course there never was a time when there were *no*
good books to read in Greek and Latin, but for
many centuries the number of Greek books in
Western Europe was very small, and many of the
best Latin writers were not known at all. But if
there had been more Greek books, they would have
been of little use to those who had not learned the
language. In Eastern Europe there were, of course,
many people who could not only read, but write and
speak Greek, as the language had never died out,
though it had changed a good deal. Still, as we
have seen, the people of Western Europe did not
think or care much about the Greeks. But when
the Turks overspread Greek-speaking lands, many
Greeks, some of them good scholars, came westward,
especially into Italy. The meetings and discussions
that went on with a view to uniting the Eastern and
Western Churches, though they did not accomplish
what was desired from them, were of use in this way,
that they opened up a path for Greek learning into
Italy and thence into France, England, and Germany.
The Italians, in spite of their sufferings and struggles,
were more clever than any other nation of Europe,

and there was arising at the courts of the princes, and among people generally who had time for reading and thinking, a great love of beautiful language and a curiosity about the life and thought of old times. So that the hunger and the food which was to satisfy it came together. It was a happy thing that more people were now able to share in the treasure that had been brought near them, because the newly invented art of printing had made books so much cheaper. The city in which Greek teachers and Greek thoughts received the warmest welcome was Florence, and the greatest friend and patron of learned men was Lorenzo dei Medici. So that his son Giovanni was brought up from his childhood in the study of the classics, and he proved a very bright pupil.

Lorenzo had several sons, and he thought it his duty to put them all in a position to make the most of themselves in life. The elder sons might be expected to obtain power and glory as statesmen or warriors. Giovanni, the youngest, he intended to make a clergyman, but he did not in the least intend that his boy should have to work his way up by his own abilities. When he was only seven years old, Giovanni received the clerical tonsure, and his father wrote to the King of France, Louis XI. (a clever man, something like Lorenzo, except that he did not care for books and pictures), asking for an abbey in France for the boy, and King Louis actually granted him one. Then the little boy abbot must receive the highest dignity in the Church next to the Papacy, he must be made a cardinal. This, too, was arranged while he was yet in his teens, after a correspondence between his father and the Pope, which Lorenzo knew well how to manage. When he was about seventeen, he went to stay in Rome and make the acquaintance of his colleagues. His father gave him good parting advice, warning him against the temptations to wickedness that he would meet with, and bidding him be genial, kindly, and modest, and not forget the interests of his family. This advice seems to have been followed. All through his life, Giovanni had a way of making himself agreeable, and there is no proof that in the very corrupt papal court he ever did anything disgraceful. He certainly cared all his life for the interests of his family, far more, we should think, than a man in such a great position ought to have cared.

After his father's death in 1492, Cardinal dei Medici and his brothers remained in Florence, and mainly directed the affairs of the city. The eldest brother, Piero, soon made himself well hated, chiefly because he always behaved as if he were lord of the city, whereas Lorenzo had wished men to think of him simply as the first of the free citizens. The cardinal was better liked, but none of the family were able to keep their position, because they were out of tune with what was noblest in the people of Florence, and, indeed, in Europe generally.

And what was that ?   The answer to this question,
if we could set it all down and take it all into our
minds, would make us see how the Medici, and
the enlightened men of their day, seemed so great
and successful for a time, and yet have since
been regarded as having failed.   They were not
enough in earnest.   They knew that in past days
there had been much ignorance, poverty, and
barbarism.   They wished to spread around them
knowledge, prosperity, and refinement.   But they
did not also realise that the late times had been bad
in a deeper sense.   There had been rudeness and
ugliness in life, that was true, but there had also
been much wickedness and corruption, and that
was much worse.   Those who took this most to
heart desired first of all that the Church should be
purified, and do its duty, and then that all Christian
people should give up quarrelling and fighting, and
should work together for the common good.   You
can see what Lorenzo thought about the work of
the Church when you consider how eager he was
to secure posts in the Church for a boy who could
not do any real clerical duty.   And you see how
much he thought of public duty when you see what
advice he gave to his son as to family interests.

Accordingly, in 1494, the Medici were driven out
of Florence.   Piero had gone out to meet the King
of France, who was on his way to invade Naples,
and he was not allowed to return to the Palace.
The cardinal tried to rouse the friends of the Medici

by riding through the city with the cry of " Palle," or " Balls." (The coat of arms of the Medici was the three balls.) But it was in vain. He threw a friar's cowl over his head and shoulders, and fled away. Immediately after, the serious thinking people in Florence followed the advice of their great preacher and teacher, Savonarola, and set up a free Christian republic which they hoped might realise a kingdom of God on earth. Perhaps they did not succeed entirely, but the experiment was worth making.

Meantime, the Medici brothers were for eighteen years exiles from their native city, though they made many attempts, helped by the Venetians, or the French, or the Pope, to force their way back. The Cardinal travelled about in Italy, Germany, and France, and widened his knowledge of life. At last they were restored by the Spanish viceroy of Naples. Piero was dead by that time, but Giuliano and the Cardinal won back the authority of their family in the State.

The year after this, Cardinal Giovanni was chosen Pope, and took the title of Leo X. He was delighted at the honour, and did not feel the heavy weight of the responsibility. "God has given us the papacy," he said, "let us enjoy it and do good to our friends." At that time, Louis XII., King of France, was very obnoxious to the papacy. But he was ready to listen to terms, and in a short time, he was persuaded to dissolve a council which he had summoned to

oppose the Pope, and to acknowledge the authority of Leo. The new Pope himself called a council at Rome, to debate on three matters : the restoration of peace, the equipment of a crusade, and the reformation of the Church. The first of these objects was to some extent, for a time, attained. The second was suggested too late. The third was beyond the power of Leo and his friends, and was being taken up, in a more summary fashion, in the countries of the North.

Leo may be said to have aimed chiefly at four things : *if possible*, he desired to bring about peace in Europe and to make the Papacy a mediating and reconciling power among warring nations ; when quarrels could not be made up, he, like his father and other clever Italian princes, liked to form alliances with the weaker against the stronger, so that the Papacy should be a gainer ; thirdly, he endeavoured to forward the interests of the Medici family in every way, carving out little principalities for his brother or nephews wherever chance allowed. And, fourthly, he wished to make Rome a dwelling-place of learned men and poets and artists even more than Florence had been in the days of Lorenzo.

In his dealings with the kings of Europe he generally succeeded fairly well. We have seen that he induced the King of France, Louis XII., to acknowledge his authority. He persuaded the kings of England and France to make peace with one another, and he pleased our King Henry VIII. by giving him the title of Defender of the Faith. After the death of Louis XII., when his young and warlike successor, Francis I., invaded Italy, Leo at first joined with the other Italians to resist him, but when Francis had won a great victory, and it seemed useless to oppose him, Leo held a friendly meeting with him, and came to an agreement with him about the government of the Church of France. Yet Leo did not like to see the French in Italy, and afterwards he made an alliance with the powerful young Emperor Charles V., who was always a rival to Francis, and was quite ready to attack the regions that the French had conquered in North Italy. The result of this alliance was that the Pope recovered Parma and Piacenza, which had belonged to the papal dominion, and afterwards to France. This was his last triumph.

I need not say much here about what he did for his family. It was greatly owing to his efforts that the Medici became more powerful than ever before, though now no one member of the family seemed capable of making the most of that power. Leo's works in Rome were partly a continuation of those of his predecessor. The greatest was the new cathedral of St. Peter's. His favourite painter, who must have worked very hard all his short life, painting on the walls of the papal palace, was Raphael, who had also, we have seen, painted the portrait of Julius II. Leo formed a kind of college at Rome for the study of Greek, and he encouraged all learned men to come to his court. He wrote once his notions on the subject as follows :— "Amongst the objects of our attention since we have been raised by Divine goodness to the pontifical dignity, and devoted to the government, and so far as it in us lies to the extension of the Christian Church, we have considered those pursuits as not the least important which lead to the promotion of literature and useful arts ; for we have been accustomed from our early years to think that nothing more excellent or more useful has been given by the Creator to mankind, if we except only the knowledge and true worship of Himself, than these studies, which not only lead to the ornament and guidance of human life, but are applicable and useful to every particular situation." [1] But sport and gorgeous spectacles delighted Leo as much as all his studies did. He did not eat or drink too much, but was not shocked to see others do so. He enjoyed life, and liked to see others enjoy it, and so far as good humour and good manners went, there was nothing to be desired about him. But the times required a man made of sterner stuff.

As one walks in the beautiful gardens on the Pincian Hill, and sees the City of Rome beneath one's feet, and beyond it the Tiber, with its ancient bridges, one's eyes travel on to a building on the other side of the river, and one can hardly take them away from the great dome of St. Peter's. One feels

[1] Roscoe's translation, "Life of Leo X," chap. xi.

that if that wonderful church is a sign for ever of the greatness of Rome, it betokens also the falling away of half Christendom from the Roman Church. For it was in order to build that cathedral that the great sale of Indulgences was carried on, which stirred the indignation of a monk in far-away Germany. Martin Luther felt that no pretext, however holy, could justify the acts of the Pope's agents in misleading and confusing ignorant people as to the nature of sin and of its consequences. At first Luther wrote respectfully to Leo, but Leo could not understand what there was to make so much ado about. He did not cause the whole dispute to be seriously discussed, nor find means to stop the evil in time. When it seemed that the breach could not be healed, he published a bull containing just the condemnation of Luther's doctrines that Luther's enemies desired. He no more understood Luther than his father had understood Savonarola. Thus it happened that the reformation in the Church which good and wise men had so long desired must be made against the authority of Rome, and in such a way as to cleave Christendom in two.

Let us look at one scene in Rome six years after Leo had passed away. Another Medici Pope, cousin to Leo, was hurrying anxiously from his palace on the other side of the Tiber to the tomb of Hadrian, which was also the fortress of St. Angelo. He wore white vestments, for he had been surprised in his chapel, and an attendant had thrown a purple cloak

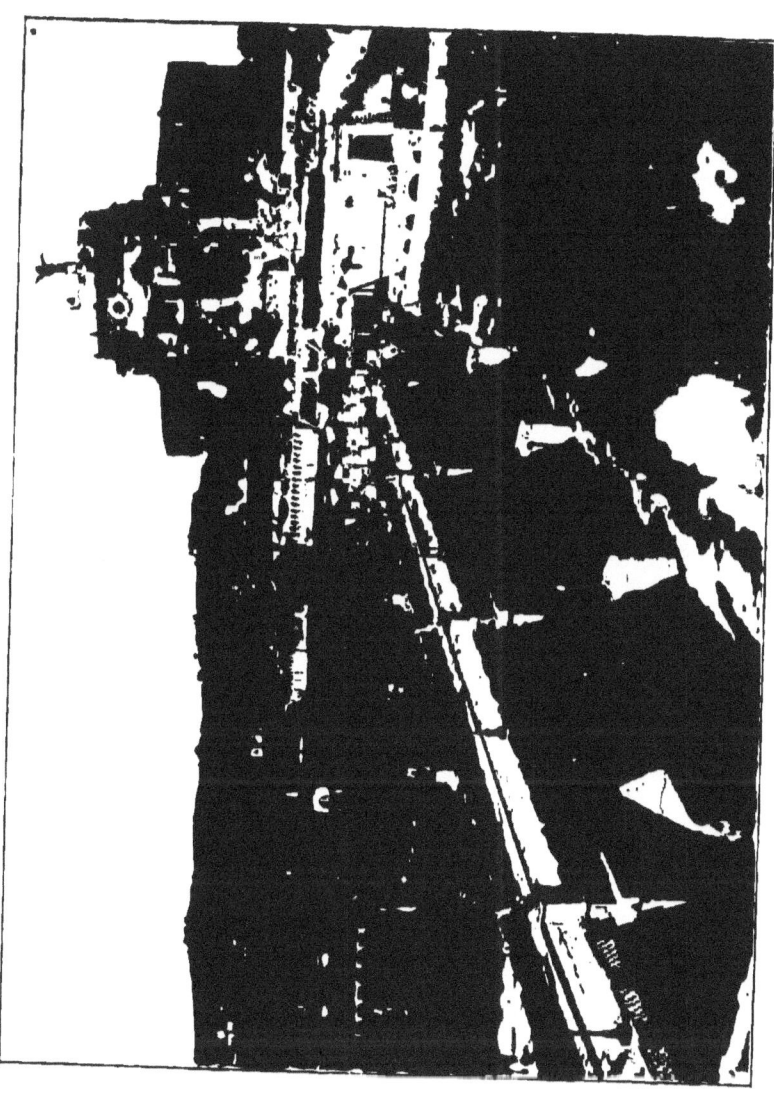

CASTLE OF ST. ANGELO, ONCE THE TOMB OF HADRIAN.

over his shoulders. Clement VII. was hastening to escape from the enemy that was attacking the city and soon poured into it, and pillaged and murdered till it suffered far worse things than Alaric or any other barbarian had brought upon it. This enemy was not heathen nor barbarian. It comprised men of three nations, Germans, Italians, and Spaniards, and was at first led by a treacherous subject of the King of France. They were supposed to belong to the Emperor Charles V., and he was supposed to be a brave champion of the Pope and of Christendom. Many of the soldiers were Lutherans, and against them none of the holy places in Rome afforded refuge.

Thus the Pope is practically a prisoner in the hands of the Emperor. Of course this state of things could not last long, but it seems to mark a time after which Rome could not in any sense seem to be the Middle of the World, as the Pope was no longer the centre of the whole Christian Church. It was while Clement was a prisoner that he was pressed by Henry VIII. of England to grant him a divorce from his wife Catherine, but Clement feared Charles, Catherine's nephew, too much to do exactly as the king wished; and all have read in their English history how this led to our king's throwing off the authority of Rome altogether, and ordering his clergy to proclaim him Supreme Head of the Church in England.

Neither Leo nor Clement was made to be a

Church reformer.   In course of time, many of the evils complained of were done away with.   But the Northern nations had been cut off from Rome for ever.   And perhaps for that very reason many from these same nations like to dwell on the last days during which men held to one Church of which Rome was the centre, and not only pious pilgrims but eager students flocked to Italy, to learn the ancient wisdom alike of the pagan philosophers and of the Fathers of the Church.

CHAPTER XIV

IT is time for us to leave Rome now, as we can no longer find there the best vantage-point for viewing the great time-procession. Great events will yet again take place within her walls. Great men will be found there from time to time. Rome will always have a history. But that history will not be so interwoven with the history of all civilised nations that by studying it we may learn all that is worth remembering in the world's history. Already, while we have been inquiring into the lives and deeds of men who have helped to make Rome famous, or shared in her glory, we have had to strain our eyes to see what was happening in cities like Florence, or even beyond the Alps. And from this time forward, it would be quite impossible to take proper account of the great events of history, or the landmarks in what people call the path of human progress, if we looked at them only as they appeared to the rulers and citizens of Rome.

The period which we have come to is that which

marks off the Middle Ages from modern times. The
line has been drawn in different ways. There are,
of course, no *lines* in real history. We only put
them in to help our memory and our understanding,
just as we put lines of latitude and longitude in our
maps. But if one wants to draw a line, I should
say, let it be so drawn that on one side we have the
times during which Rome was, in some kind of
sense, the Middle of the World, and on the other the
times in which it is clear to everybody that there *is*
no such middle point to be found in Rome or
anywhere else. But we shall not be able to see the
distinction unless I have fulfilled the promise made
in my first chapter. Let us see whether our views
at some points which I wanted you to see clearly,
with a hurried glance at what lies between, have
made us realise in what different senses, from the
days of Augustus till those of the Medici Popes,
Rome has been a real centre round which all the
world might seem to move.

First, then, we have seen how Rome was the
centre of government for all the nations about
which our history is concerned — the political
middle of the world. She had, you will remember, obtained, even while a republic, a position as
judge and arbitrator among many peoples, and had
made many countries into *provinces*, governed by
rulers sent from Rome. But the Republic was
breaking down under the task of governing the
world, when the Cæsars came, first Julius and then

Augustus, to establish an Empire united in peace and
in obedience to the First Man in the City of Rome.
We have seen also how much the early emperors
did to beautify Rome and to make the City worthy
of her proud position. So firmly was the Roman
dominion established in the Provinces, that during
the reigns of bad, or even half-mad, emperors—like
Nero—power and order were, on the whole, fairly
well kept. We have seen the great soldier-emperor,
Trajan, listening to speeches in his honour delivered
in the Roman Senate, and the never-tired traveller,
Hadrian, resting for a brief period in the City in
the pauses of his journeys east and west. But
after their time, Rome grows less able to struggle
against the difficulties which beset her more and
more thickly. We find the emperors less and less
of Romans—we have seen Syrian ladies practically
ruling the Empire; and meanwhile the barbarians,
are seeking settlements within Roman provinces—
like those against whom young Alexander Severus
had to take the field, and there are mutinies of the
soldiers, such as the one in which that unfortunate
boy lost his life.

But, meanwhile, Rome is acquiring a great name
and far-reaching influence of a quite different
kind. For she is looked upon as the *one* great
centre of the Christians, of the small sect that
Nero had begun to persecute, and that Alexander
and his mother had learned to respect. At length
the Empire itself becomes Christian, but not till it

had lost its old character, and become a monarchy which does not pretend to be anything else. At about the same time, the Emperor Constantine founds a city which is to be a kind of new Rome, at the entrance to the Black Sea. This, one would have thought, might have put an end to the greatness of Rome. But instead of that, we find Rome commanding more and more respect in her new character as the chief of Christian cities, the holy place where St. Peter and St. Paul had suffered martyrdom, and her bishop soon comes to be regarded as the head of the Christian Church, at least in the West, and can have his own way more effectually than if the Emperor were always by his side. We notice how the barbarians, as they swarm down into the Roman world, though they have no scruples against pillaging and destroying on all sides, feel nevertheless quite overawed when they approach the City of Rome, and how the wisest of them come to the conclusion that it would be better to copy, as far as possible, the civilised ways of the Romans, and even to work under the Romans and acknowledge the Emperor as supreme, than to try to root out the Roman name.

The worthiest attempt made by a barbarian leader to put young blood into the old body is that of Theodoric the Ostrogoth. If he had succeeded, it is not impossible that since he himself generally lived at Ravenna, and his palace and churches and tomb were there, there *might* have been two capitals

in Italy, one sacred and one civil, as there have been
in Russia and many other countries. But while
Ravenna would have been the civil capital for Italy,
Rome would have been the sacred capital of the
World. After the death of Theodoric and the failure
of his successors, we have no emperor or king in
Rome or in Italy, and the Popes seem to stand at
the head of the Church and the World in the eyes
of at least some of the conquering barbarians. But
the Popes find themselves in sore straits between
Eastern emperors and half-heretic Lombards, until
they call in their great Frankish champion, and on
Christmas Day, 800, the Roman Empire is revived
in Rome, and becomes the Holy Roman Empire.

Then, indeed, no one in Christian Europe (except
of course, most of the subjects of the Emperor
who reigns at Constantinople) can help thinking
of Rome as the Middle of the World, for it is the
city of Popes and Emperors, who are set over
all Christian people to govern and defend them.
But Popes and Emperors, after a time, do not agree
as to what the rightful share of each one is in the
government of the Christian world. The Emperors,
too, have lands to see to far away, and cannot be
often in Rome. It is a time of great suffering and
strife and corruption. Then some of the Popes try
to reform matters, and think that reform can only
be accomplished by putting the ruler of the Church
above the ruler of the world. Thence comes the
great conflict between Hildebrand and Henry IV.

Meantime strong kingdoms are being founded in Europe which own no obedience to the Emperor, and object to the high claims of the Pope. We have seen how King Philip the Fair is so far successful as to induce the Pope, after the death of Boniface VIII., to leave Rome for Avignon, and live under his protection, thus beginning the " Babylonish Captivity."

But in spite of all this, the feeling remains that Rome is, or ought to be, the Middle of the World, and for a short time the Tribune Rienzi tries to revive her power, by uniting the traditions of her ancient freedom and glory with her claims as possessing the throne of St. Peter. Rienzi fails, and after the "Captivity" is over, there is the yet more disgraceful spectacle of two rival Popes, one at Rome and one at Avignon, each claiming supremacy over the whole Church. The schism is healed by a Council, but the Popes, who again live in Rome and are acknowledged by the nations of Europe, have to strive so hard to recover and to keep the cities and districts belonging to the Papacy in Italy, that people come to look on them more as Italians than as rulers set above all nations.

When Europe, and especially Italy, wakes up to take a fresh interest in books, art, and most of all in the works of ancient times, some of the Popes share in the movement and try to lead it, making Rome and its court an example of refinement and culture for all who flock thither from all parts of the world. But these Popes seemed to have forgotten the religious side of their office altogether, and also to have given up the hope of establishing unity and concord in the countries which obeyed them.

Meantime, men are coming forward, especially in Germany, who care most of all about those things to which the Popes are indifferent, and who think that splendour and worldly greatness are not worth considering in comparison with religious sincerity. These Popes are not in sympathy with the Reformation, and thus they lose the obedience of many German and all English speaking peoples. The Popes of the next century set a far higher value on their duties, as heads of Christendom, to the cause of Christianity and truth, but the breach was already made. Rome, as seat of the Papacy, was not looked up to by all. Many Protestants regarded it as the wickedest of cities, Great Babylon. Nor was Rome any longer the seat of the Emperors. Charles V. was crowned in Italy, but not in Rome. The great powers divided up the Italian states among themselves, and Rome was for a while left to the Pope—an Italian principality like many others, but generally the worst governed of all.

But what is Rome *now*? Apart from her wonderful history, is there nothing about her which attracts travellers to her and makes her even now to rank as one of the great cities of the world? Yes, Rome is now important in two ways — as chief centre of the Roman Church and as capital of the Italian kingdom.

The Pope has, within the recollection of some of us, ceased to hold power as a ruling prince, but, seeing how vast is the number of people belonging to the Church of which he is the head, he must always have a good deal of power and importance, even in the eyes of people who do not belong to his Church. It is often necessary that a king or prince who has Roman Catholic subjects should refer to the Pope and ask his advice as to any difficulties that may arise in the dealings of his government with them. And occasionally, in our own times, when some difficult question which has something to do with morals and religion is weighing on men's consciences, the Pope has uttered his mind about it in a general letter, which is respected by all Roman Catholics, and in many cases by those who belong to other churches. For example, the present Pope, not long ago, wrote a general letter on the way in which workmen and their employers ought to act towards one another. He did not issue commands, but gave good advice, and he is in a position to make sure that his advice is at least listened to.

And again, Rome is the capital of Italy. Italy never had a capital, in the ordinary sense, till a quite short time ago. If you want to learn a great

deal of history in an interesting way, you might set
to work to find out how the *capitals* of the great
countries of Europe came to be such. It might
not seem very hard to find out how London came
to be the capital of England, but you would come
across more that was interesting if you asked how
St. Petersburg became the capital of Russia, and
Constantinople of Turkey, and Athens of Greece,
and Rome of Italy. Italy, as we have seen, was
not a separate country in the Middle Ages nor in
the times that followed. It is quite within my
recollection (though I am not very old) how the
Italians determined to be united, and found a hero
to lead them—Garibaldi. The kingdom of Naples
and Sicily, which had been abominably governed,
was taken from its former kings and joined to
parts of North Italy under the King of Sardinia,
who had been accustomed to rule according to
law, and believed in *government along with the
people*. Victor Emmanuel thus became the first
King of Italy, but for a time the Pope still had
Rome, and the Emperor of the French kept
soldiers there to protect him. In the year 1870,
however, when the French were fighting against
the Germans and could not spare soldiers for
Italy, the Italians took possession of the City and
made it the capital of their free kingdom. The
Pope might still live in the Vatican, on the other
side of the Tiber. Of course, the Italians were
proud and delighted to have the Great City for their

18

capital, but there was much bitter feeling between those who wished to keep as much power as possible for the Papacy and those who believed in the new monarchy. So far as the last Pope who ruled in Rome, Pius IX., and the first king are concerned, they were not on easy terms till near the end of their lives, but then the breach between them was healed. They both lay dying within a short distance of one another, and friendly messages passed between them, Pope Pius declaring his sorrow that this fatal illness of his prevented him from going to give the dying king his blessing.

Yet it seems, perhaps, a great come-down for Rome which has been the Middle of the World to have come to be the capital of an ordinary kingdom. And has she not left a place empty? Would it not be a grand thing, nowadays, if there were *some* power that was raised above all nations and could help them to make up all their quarrels? Should we not feel more brotherly towards one another if there were one spot on earth to which we all looked as to a kind of home and refuge, where the oppressed might seek justice, and where tyrants might be reproved for their crimes? Above all, has not Europe suffered from being divided into so many churches, and from religious disputes and controversies and differences that make good men cease to regard one another as fellow-Christians? Would it not be a de-

lightful idea to have all nations bound into one
Roman Empire again, with some allowance made
for the natural differences, and love of independence in various countries, and to have one
Church in ·which all Christian people might find
a home ?

Yes, it would be a delightful idea, but it has
never been realised, and probably never will be.
The difference between our time and the Middle
Ages is that in those times people aimed at this
kind of unity and did not reach it, and nowadays
we do not aim at it at all. When there was one
Church (setting aside the Greek), there were perpetual conflicts going on within it. When the
Emperor and the Pope claimed the right of
making peace among all people, wars went on
just the same. But nevertheless, the thought that
all men ought to form one brotherhood, that wars
and fightings should be avoided whenever possible,
that no government has a right to oppress any
people under its sway, that men who think differently on religious matters ought to combine
together to try to make the world better, as far
as they possibly can — these ideas are, perhaps,
more easily taken in and sometimes acted upon by
us because the world once realised its unity by
having a middle in Rome.

Or you may put the thought in another way, if
you like to make an allegory. Have you not often,
when winding a ball of wool or of string, put your

finger, or a bit of paper, in the middle, and slipped it out when the ball had taken shape enough to do without it ? So you may fancy that as God was winding the skein of the world's history, He put Rome in the middle of the ball, and then, when it was no longer wanted there, He slipped it out, to use it for another purpose.

The unity of mankind, the brotherhood among all nations, does not depend upon our all being under one government, either in things of the flesh or of the spirit. Yet those who had known the Roman Empire were able to proclaim that unity the most clearly, and their words will last for ever. It was the Apostle Paul, a Roman citizen himself, who told the Roman Christians that they were " one body in Christ and every one members one of another." And it was the best and wisest of the Roman Emperors who, when weary of having to work with ungrateful, envious, and unsocial men, braced himself to do his best, even with them, by the thought : " We are made for co-operation, like feet, like hands, like eyelids, like the rows of the upper and lower teeth. To act against one another, then, is contrary to Nature."

THE END.

UNWIN BROTHERS, THE GRESHAM PRESS, WOKING AND LONDON